COUNTDOWN TO DOOMSDAY!

He turned to face me, those strange eyes on mine. "You begin to perceive the ultimate danger of the spores being released. We have no idea how adaptable they are to the climates of Earth. They could be killed by the first frost . . . but that seems unlikely. Then again, they could be killed by certain bacteria or other microorganisms here. Or . . ." The glint in his eye positively glowed. "They could mean the end. **The end of life on earth as we know it** . . . You begin to understand. You begin to see. As the world will begin to see . . ." He looked up at the clock on the wall. "Around . . . oh . . . **twelve hours from now.**"

From The Nick Carter Killmaster Series

Revenge of the Generals
The Man Who Sold Death
Temple of Fear
The Liquidator
The Nichovev Plot
The Judas Spy
Time Clock of Death
Under the Wall
The Jerusalem File
The Filthy Five
The Sign of the Cobra
Six Bloody Summer Days
The Z Document
The Ultimate Code
The Green Wolf Connection
The Katmandu Contract
The Night of the Avenger
Beirut Incident

NICK CARTER IS IT!

"Nick Carter out-Bonds James Bond."
—Buffalo Evening News

"Nick Carter is America's #1 espionage agent."
—Variety

"Nick Carter is razor-sharp suspense."
—King Features

"Nick Carter is extraordinarily big."
—Bestsellers

"Nick Carter has attracted an army of addicted readers . . . the books are fast, have plenty of action and just the right degree of sex . . . Nick Carter is the American James Bond, suave, sophisticated, a killer with both the ladies and the enemy."
—The New York Times

Dedicated to the Men of the Secret Services of the United States of America

A Killmaster Spy Chiller

THE DOOMSDAY SPORE

A DIVISION OF CHARTER COMMUNICATIONS INC.
A GROSSET & DUNLAP COMPANY

THE DOOMSDAY SPORE

Charter Books
A Division of Charter Communications, Inc.
A Grosset & Dunlap Company
360 Park Avenue South
New York, New York 10010

Manufactured in the United States of America

ONE

I STOPPED ON the top step, the fiddle case under my arm, feeling like an idiot. "Terence, my boy," I said, "what if somebody asks me to play this thing?"

Terry Considine stood beside me staring up at the huge double doors of the Italian Embassy. Chuckling, he turned to me and said, "Then you're in big trouble, Nick old pal. Haven't you looked inside the case?"

"No," I snapped, embarrassed that I let something get by me. "What's there?"

"Just a few sandwiches. The word is, the Embassy doesn't have the best cooks this season. His Excellency seems to be well-known for tight pockets and a numb palate. I heard he called some agency for a cheap short-order cook."

"Jesus," I mumbled, becoming irritated, "ring the bell."

As Terry pressed on the small black buzzer, he gestured at the case in his right hand. "I suppose I didn't tell you about my two years at the New England Conservatory. I can actually play . . ."

"*Sh-sh!* Sounds like someone's coming."

Just then one of large doors cracked open slightly. "Musicians," I said, peering into the darkness. It was then that I noticed Terry was still babbling.

". . . . The unfortunate thing is that I only learned the scale in one key, and I only picked up one tune; then I had to give the damned horn back."

Now both doors swung open and—interestingly—we were greeted by a Spaniard! He shooed us in, making sure we took the service door to the right. I gave him the expected "yassuh" and scuttled out of sight to wait for Terry.

"So far, so good," he said as he looked around. "Now what?"

"Take this goddamn fiddle case," I ordered, "and give the backstage area a once-over. Check for everything. Shake down everybody."

"For what?"

"Didn't you get to talk to Hawk?"

"No. The phone line where he caught me wasn't secure."

I looked him up and down quickly. Terry was big, redheaded, second-generation Irish, and as tough a customer as AXE had ever thrown me as a backup man. Sizing him up, I applauded David Hawk's judgment in sending him along. Terry could do everything . . . except fold four cards to an inside straight. He had every strength God had ever given the Irish, and damn few of the weaknesses.

"Shake 'em down," I said, "for anything that could kill anybody. Because if we don't find whoever the hell it is and disarm him in . . ." I looked at my watch. ". . . In fifteen minutes."

He groaned.

"You've got it," I said. "A major assassination. Triple priority. Hawk said the call came from . . ."

"From Sixteen Hundred Pennsylvania Avenue. Jesus, Mary an' Joseph. And who is going to get the honor of being sent to the Saints?"

"Nobody has the slightest idea. All we know is that it's serious as hell."

"God almighty. Any idea of how it's going to be done?"

"We don't know another thing. It could be an icepick up somebody's ass or it could be a satchelful of something that'll blow up everything, and everybody, between the National Geographic

Building and the Maryland line."

"I knew I should have taken that job playing tight end for the Redskins. And we have how long to stop it?"

"Fourteen—no thirteen minutes."

I started to add the wry comment to speed the parting guest, but he was way ahead of me. All I saw was his broad back disappearing around a corner.

I did my own bit of groaning when I walked into the big reception room of the Embassy. The place was crawling with people. And as I looked around, identifying one face after another, my heart sank at the task.

They weren't the sort of faces you'd know unless you were pretty well plugged into the Capital. Nobody knows the diplomats, for the most part, except people who have reason to know them. But—damn it to hell—*every* ambassador of *every* country outside the Third World crowd was there. I ticked them off: France . . . Germany . . . the Soviet Union . . . Canada . . . Australia . . . Sweden . . . and, of course, His Excellency Sir Frederick Thornton, K.C.B.E., Ambassador of Great Britain. Guest of Honor at the party. An elder statesman who was celebrating his thirtieth year in the British foreign service. Yeah, there he was, jawing with the Cultural Attache from West Germany.

Someone in the room was scheduled to get himself jerked up to Jesus in eleven minutes. And we had no idea who. Or why. Or how.

I was just about to go backstage and help Terry when I spotted a familiar face heading my way. Red-haired, red-bearded; wearing—even in these circumstances, with soup and fish *de rigueur* on all sides—a suit that looked like he'd slept in it. And sporting a wry and sharp-eyed variety of the well-known coprophagous grin.

"Robert Franks," I said.

"Howdy." The voice was low and didn't carry as Bob Franks slipped up to my side. "I'm alarmed. You wouldn't be here," he said, "unless some sort of shit were about to hit some sort of fan."

Bob's status had never been quite so clearly defined as I'd have liked. He'd had a very high clearance once. For all we knew he might well have one now. He worked whenever he chose as a sort of free-lance consultant to anyone and everyone in the Capital. We'd found out we could trust him with the damned little we approved of having him find out. The rest . . . well, he had a sharp eye and there wasn't much time.

"You got it," I said. "In ten minutes the clock is going to run out for somebody here. If you've seen anything . . ."

"Hmmmm." He fiddled with his beard. "I'll think about that. You've got somebody backstage?"

"Yeah. But who's there?"

"The entertainment. Which consists of the

twelve stalwart strings of the Miniver Cheevy Society's Baroque orchestra, courtesy of your humble servant. . . ."

"Yeah. And?"

"And, of course, the main attraction. The opening program of the first American tour of The Great Marconi, Master of Mystery. He's an illusionist and escape artist. The high spot of his program will be a stunt he's performed at every court in Europe. He bought it from the Houdini estate. They lock him inside an iron cylinder—padlocks, chains, the works. Then they suspend the cylinder in the air, frozen inside a giant cake of ice. The cylinder remains in full view the whole time. And by God if the son of a bitch doesn't. . . . Hey, Nick."

"Yeah?"

"The president was supposed to be at this thing. Have you seen him?"

"No. They've warned him off. But I just spotted the Secretary of Defense."

"Jesus."

"You're sure you haven't seen anything?"

"No, I—hey, wait."

"What?"

"The new paparazzo."

"New what?"

"There's a news photographer here I don't recognize."

Bob hung out with television photographers; they were regulars at a bar on Connecticut where he had a friendly arrangement with the bartender—who just happened to play the viola in Bob's band when he was off duty.

"Can you point him out?" I asked with some interest.

"Hmmm . . . I don't see him right now," Franks said as he scanned the crowded room. "He may have gone backstage to get a shot of our magician friend."

"What does he look like?"

"Sort of a little, pushfaced guy. Looks like a young version of . . . aw, goddamn . . . you remember Jimmy Gleason? The actor? Used to play prizefight managers?"

"Yeah. Hey, if you see him find me. Don't tackle him yourself."

"Nick, I . . . ."

"I'm not kidding. God knows what's in his camera. We don't know anything about the method. It may be loaded with gelignite. Or . . . ."

"Oh, wow. Well, there goes my string orchestra."

"There goes international relations. Everybody in the whole damn diplomatic world is here. India . . . Israel . . . Turkey . . . Iran. . . ."

"You're a little bundle of joy. I'll keep an eye out."

"You do that." I slipped through the curtain at the end of the big room, trying to look musical.

There was a sort of hall between the green room

and auditorium, and in it Bob's fiddlers walked back and forth, playing scales, playing Kreutzer, warming up the fingers. A lone cellist sat, instrument between his knees, abstractedly playing a boogie-woogie bass pattern *pizzicato* on his cello. Behind the players, burly roughies were moving the illusionist's gear into place. This was block-and-tackle equipment, weighing hundreds of pounds. It looked as though they were getting ready to drill an oil well in the middle of the ballroom, and all they had to do was roll the damned derrick inside.

I pushed past a fiddler playing Joe Venuti licks and went into the green room. Terry looked up from the frisk he was giving the second of two roughies who had been helping move the equipment. The first regarded him with the sort of look you give somebody you're thinking of giving a fat lip.

"Nick," he said, looking over at me. "No soap so far. These guys are clean. I . . ."

"Now," said a voice from behind a screen in the corner. A dapper little man stepped out from behind the shoji. He wore the traditional magician's tailcoat and red-lined black cape, white gloves, and an amused smile. The black wig and Mandrake moustache were patently phony, and probably weren't meant to look any other way. "Now if you gentlemen are through."

"You're Marconi?" I said.

"At your service, *signore*."

"Oh, cut out the *signore* stuff, hey?" Terry told

him with a grin. "Nick, the Great Marconi is a Mick from County Kerry. His father had a feud once with a great uncle of mine, he says. Not that I'd know the Blarney Stone from Plymouth Rock unless I had money bet on it."

"Nice to meet you," I said. I held out my hand. Marconi winced and pulled his hand away.

"I—I never shake hands," he said. "I'm sorry. Some parts of my act . . . they require a great delicacy with the fingers . . . you understand the precautions I have to take. They are, after all, my living."

"Sure," I said. I turned to Terry. "Five god-damn minutes. No, four. You've frisked Marconi?"

"Yeah. And I checked the equipment. Nothing there."

"I got a tip from out front. Somebody's spotted a news photographer who doesn't seem to belong . . ."

"Little guy with a lot more chin than nose? Balding on top? Wearing a coat that looks a couple sizes too large?"

"Could be. You've seen him?"

"He just went out the door. Heading for the john, he said . . ."

I didn't wait for him to finish. I was gone, at a run. There was a big guy, apparently one of the roughies, coming my way.

"Hey," I said. "Did you see a little guy with a camera?"

"Camera?" he asked.

I didn't see what was in his hand as I ran past. Whatever it was knocked me to my knees, then my face. As I tried to rise somebody hit me again.

I shook my head.

Music was playing. Tchaikovsky's *Serenade For Strings*.

Music!

I was too late! The performance had started. I got my hands under me and shoved to get up, trying to shake the cobwebs out of my eyes, my brain.

Up ahead of me in the dim hallway some people were fighting. Wrestling. I could hear groans. Someone was hit and went down. And now I could see two others bending over him, hitting him again.

I got my feet under me and charged. I hit the bigger of the two amidships and tackled him. He went down, rolling.

"Nick!" Terry said. I wanted to answer, but the man I'd tackled caught me a good one over the eye. I blinked—there wasn't time for anything in the way of subtlety. I bulled into him as he tried to rise. He slammed against the wall and came back at me, fists going. I ducked one, barely slipped another, and gave him a nice one in the short ribs. I thought I felt something give. He groaned and swung again, grunting in pain as he did.

"Come back here, you little bastard." Terry

said behind me. I could hear feet pounding down the hall, toward the side door. Two pairs of feet. The photographer's small ones—and those big brogans of Terence Considine, AXE Agent N21.

Then the guy I was waltzing with missed a roundhouse aimed at my chin. As he did so he left himself wide open. I snapped a left hook across a few inches of space. He went down as if he'd run into a train.

My own head went up.

Down the hall Terry caught the Jimmy Gleason look-alike. They grappled in a pool of light near the side door. Terry pulled the guy's coat open; it tore away.

His chest was covered with sticks. Fused sticks of dynamite.

There was a sudden flash.

In that marble hall it sounded like bloody hell. And the shock wave knocked me for a loop as the ceiling caved in. The side door—they told me later—landed half a block away on Columbia Road. What was left of it.

I sat up slowly. And then clawed wildly at my coat.

It was covered with flecks of blood . . . and little pieces of flesh.

Pieces of the guy who looked like Jimmy Gleason.

Pieces of Terry Considine.

TWO

I BRUSHED SOME of the gore off me; there was something solid there, something black. Absently, I shoved it in my shirt pocket.

Down the hall there was a gaping hole, letting out the stale air of the Embassy, letting in the stale air of the District. Something had caught fire from the blast and was smoldering.

There wasn't much left of either guy. And now, as I looked, the clothing of one of them began to burn. I couldn't tell which one of them it was.

Wake up, Carter. You've got a concussion, and

yes, that is blood from your nose running down your upper lip into your mouth.

I looked around. There was the guy I'd creamed with the sucker punch only moments before, trying to struggle to his feet.

"No, you don't," I said. I scrambled after him, grabbed one foot as he rose, twisted, and dumped him on his nose. "Hey," I said. "You stay put. I need you . . . ."

He was nice and quick on the draw. The leg I'd pulled drew back and caught me one over the eye as I moved forward, and I went end over end. It bought him enough time to scramble to his feet just as the door opened and people started pouring out into the hall.

He was a quick thinker, this one. "Help!" he said. "That man there . . . he's the one . . . he's the man who did it . . . ."

"Stop him!" I said. "Somebody stop him!" But damn it, they chose him to believe. He had the advantage of looking like everybody else. Soup and fish, most of it clean. Me, I was all over gore. A couple of burly lads from the Embassy staff bore down on me. Our little friend—all two hundred pounds of him—disappeared into the crowd.

"Hey, damn it," I said. "You're letting him get away . . . ."

"Cuidado," said the one on the left. *"Creo que tiene una pistola."* He and his friend advanced on me one step at a time. The hall was full of people by now, and the noise was considerable.

I didn't have time to show my credentials as the man on the right moved in. I swept his hand down, spun him around, twisted his arm high behind his back, and literally threw him at the other guy. Then I made a rush for it.

A few of them had the good sense to get out of my way. The rest I bowled over, and without the smallest twinge of conscience. And damned if the guy I'd tackled in the hall wasn't still in there, trying to look like somebody who had a right to be there. I looked around. "Bob! Bob Franks! Close that goddamn door! Don't let him out . . . ."

The guy was making a break for it right then and there. Bob was up front trying to swing the door shut. He looked around in time to dive for the floor as the big guy pulled a snubnosed revolver and squeezed off a round in his direction. Franks—a lot more agile than I'd have given him credit for—rolled deftly behind a huge overstuffed chair and was safe for the moment. But me? Our friend turned and let one go at me . . . and then I broke my rule about showing iron on the sacred diplomatic ground. I reached inside my coat for Wilhelmina—a factory-perfect 9mm Luger slightly older than I was, and just as deadly.

"Drop it!" I commanded.

Just as I was about to put him on ice until the authorities could arrive, a young blonde came through the door. He grabbed her by the neck immediately, and she let out a frightened, ear-piercing scream.

"All right," he yelped, a tremor in his voice, his eyes focused directly on me. He had a slight accent, but one I couldn't readily distinguish. Some part of England or Canada that I didn't know, perhaps.

"All right," he said again. "If anybody so much as moves a muscle, the lady gets it in the head. Just like that . . . ."

The room was suddenly very empty of people. Apparently they assumed he meant they weren't supposed to move any direction but backward. My fingers itched on Wilhelmina's grip.

"You, Carter." he said, his voice becoming more steady.

How the hell did he know me?

Inside my head an alarm buzzer went off and rang like blazes.

"Drop the gun straight down. Don't try anything. Just let it go, and then I'll back right out of here . . ."

"Leave the lady behind," I said. "She hasn't done anything."

"Sorry," he said. The lady began to scream again. A big hand went over her mouth. "Not a chance," he told me. "Insurance."

My hand was still on the gun. My fingers were loose, though. "Not a chance indeed," I said. "Let her go right now . . . or I'll shoot right over her—and accurately. If you know me well enough to know my name you know that much about me. She's not big enough for you to hide behind.

There'll always be some part of you I can hit—and from which you can bleed to death. An artery in the leg, for instance. I . . ."

There was a commotion outside in the foyer. A bullhorn bellowed: *"All right, come on out. The place is surrounded."*

"That's the SWAT team," I said. "Special Weapons and Tactics. Any one of them can disarm you and cut you in little pieces with his bare hands. The only thing that's keeping me from doing it myself is the passing thought that the lady might get her hairdo mussed in the process. And that isn't going to happen. You're going to go quietly. You remember the SLA shootout in Los Angeles? Well, these guys are six times as tough."

Out of the corner of my eye I saw Bob Franks edging to the near side of the huge chair he was hiding behind. He had a heavy glass ashtray in one hand. I kept my eyes on the gunman, but when I shook my head I had Franks in my mind. "No," I said. "Don't do it. It's too dangerous . . . ."

But there was Franks, damn it, chewing on his red moustache, edging into place. I knew just what he was going to do. He was as deadly in a dart game as I was at the small-arms range. "No," I said, my voice aimed at the gunman but my words aimed at Franks. "It isn't worth it. You'll just get killed."

Behind the gunman a battering ram banged heavily at the door. His hand went to his mouth. The cops broke down the door, and I was just in time to grab the lady as she fell to the floor in a faint. Behind her her assailant slumped into a heap. Behind his inert body the cops kicked in the door and jumped into the room, brandishing M16s. I sighed, dropped Wilhelmina to the floor, and put my hands up.

Of course, he was dead when they got to him. Whatever he'd taken, it was quick and final. And there went our chance of finding out who he was, and who he represented. The cops put the frisk on me netting three good friends of mine: Wilhelmina, the Luger; Pierre, my little gas bomb; and Hugo, the peerless long-bladed shiv I keep up one sleeve. They were about to put the cuffs on me when the ambassador came to my rescue.

"No, no," he said. "Please. This man . . . he saved my wife. . . ."

Well, that was some entree. It took some more explaining, and finally it took having the cop in charge of the SWAT unit call a certain number down on the Mall. I watched as his eyebrows went up and the tone of his voice became quiet and respectful. He hung up at last and looked over at me with new eyes. "Sorry," he said. "Under the circumstances we couldn't take any chances. I. . . ."

"I understand," I said, and I did. Special firepower or no, he was just the cop on the spot, unable to tell the home team from the bad guys without a program.

We set up a roll call in the foyer, lining everybody up, checking credentials. Then we ran another on the servants. After we got the list done the lieutenant started checking it against the guest list. I went back into the other room, having liberated my three lethal little friends and stowed them.

Bob Franks was arguing with a cop. The cop wanted to know just what Franks was doing here. He wasn't conducting the band, was he?

"He's okay. I said. "Ask Lt. Agnelli, up front. He'll vouch for me. I'll vouch for Franks."

"Well . . . ." Keeping one eye on us, he sidled back to the open door where Agnelli, the SWAT leader, was calling off names.

"Thanks," Bob Franks said. "I think I'm going to stick to booking the band as live classical Muzak behind art-show openings. I'm getting a little long in the tooth for all this razzle-dazzle."

"You damn fool, you almost got yourself killed. Didn't you hear me warning you off? If the cops hadn't busted down the door just then . . . ."

"On the other hand, that so-and-so took a potshot at me. Nobody does that to . . ." Franks's face had suddenly turned stark white.

"What is it?" I asked. "You look like you've just seen a ghost."

The color came back to his ruddy face a little at a time. "It's not the ghosts I'm seeing but the ones I ain't. That goddamn magician. He's been up there on that derrick, locked inside that steel cylinder, frozen inside that cake of ice for thirty-five minutes. With enough air for about ten . . . ."

He beat me to the winch. The apparatus was secured with a mean-looking knot; I whipped out Hugo and sliced through the heart of it like Alexander the Great at Gordium. Bob went to work on the block-and-tackle arrangement that held the dripping cake of ice high above its tank in the middle of the big auditorium. "The ice." he said. "There's a big sledge over there . . . ."

The sledge was one of those big-headed wooden monsters you see at carnivals; people used them to pound in the tent stakes. I hefted it and took a big backswing. The sledge went way up . . . then down . . . and the ice smashed into a million pieces!

"Well, for God's sake," I said, "The damn thing's hollow."

"Of course it is," Franks said. "I saw the rehearsal. There's no time to actually freeze him in there. They used a hollowed-out cake of ice, made by freezing big blocks together in an igloo pattern. It's still a pretty spectacular stunt."

"I'll bet. Where are those damn keys?"

"That must be them over here. Here, catch."

"Okay," I grabbed them in midair and went to work on the locks that held the cylinder shut.

"No," he said. "Roll the thing over on its side so we can get the poor devil out. Not that I think it's going to make much difference by now. He can't still be alive, Houdini trick or no. The air ran out inside that thing a long time back, I'm sure."

In a moment we had him. We rolled him out on his back. The face was familiar and the guy behind it was dead. Only he hadn't died from asphyxiation. That conclusion had something to do with the eight-inch dagger protruding from the middle of his chest. The blood stained his evening clothes and soaked through to the black-and-red magician's cloak he wore over them.

It also stained the back of the white paper through which the dagger had been thrust into his chest. I read it through just as the cops hove into view, telling me to be careful not to touch anything.

The blood soaking through the paper brought out a shamrock watermark—and the following message:

And will Ireland then be free?
Says the Shan Van Vocht;
Will Ireland then be free?
Says the Shan Van Vocht;
Yes! Ireland shall be free.
From the centre to the sea;
Then hurrah for Liberty!
Says the Shan Van Vocht.

UNION OR DEATH
Captain Moonlight

Only the gent whose chest it was decorating wasn't the dapper little magician I'd met backstage. But I knew the face. It belonged to Sir Frederick Thornton, K.C.B.E., Ambassador of Great Britain to the United States.

The magician? Not a sign of him anywhere!

THREE

TWO DAYS LATER David Hawk and I stood on a hillside in Arlington watching the man in the turned-around collar say the last words over Terry Considine. It was a gray day, with low clouds that had National Airport socked in, and as the priest got off the last few Latin words it started to rain.

I looked around, feeling a sudden chill. There weren't many of us: Hawk and myself, and a girl Terry'd dated, but who had broken off their engagement when she found out something of what he did for a living. I wondered what she was thinking now. Her face was somber and drawn. Maybe she'd lost something she hadn't known the value of until now.

There weren't any other AXE people there. The business doesn't stop just because one of us buys the farm.

I looked at Hawk. "I think," I said, "that in the best of all possible worlds I'd skip the part where they start shoveling the dirt on him. If you don't mind." I thought a moment and then added, "Sir."

Hawk looked around at me. His gaze landed on my tie first, then worked its way up to my face. "Yeah," he said in that gruff voice. "Let's go."

His face looked a little odd without a stogie in it, being worried the way a pit bull worries a rat. There was a sour note there that made his usual less-than-enthusiastic tone sound like the tinkling of Christmas bells beside it. He jammed his hands into his pockets and strolled away. I caught up. Hawk had actually had a suit pressed for the funeral, and here it was getting sticky with one of those greasy Potomac drizzles.

We followed the path down the hill. Neither of us said anything, all the way to Hawk's car—a ten-year-old bucket of bolts that looked like disaster on wheels and would do a hundred and forty on the roughest roads rural Virginia could devise. He took out the keys and looked at them with disgust. "Here," he said handing them to me. "You're the active agent—you drive."

I took us down the hill to the turnaround and we went across the bridge past the Lincoln Memorial. Hawk suggested that I turn there and cut over by the Tidal Basin. The drizzle was knocking the last of the cherry blossoms off the trees. The city looked dismal, and the cold Potomac fog was getting into my bones. *Some spring I thought!*

"Pull over," Hawk said, his tone indicating something was on his mind.

I stopped under a stand of wilted-looking cherry trees and parked the car. As I turned off the ignition, the car made such rumbling sounds I expected it would collapse any minute. Yet, as I was driving it, I could feel the damn thing purr; it was amazing. I was still puzzling over the car when Hawk finally spoke.

Looking straight ahead, he said curtly, "Okay, you have something to say. Say it!"

"Yes, sir." I got out one of my custom-made cigarettes and lit it, giving Hawk a light for the cigar that had miraculously appeared between his back teeth. "I . . . let's say I'm pissed off. I've been led up the garden path by someone and faked out of position, and it has cost me not only a mission, but a good friend as well. I want to finish this assignment." I blew smoke out into the already polluted air of Washington. "Sir," I added between clenched teeth.

"Okay," Hawk said matter-of-factly. "You've got it."

I was just ready to argue with him, and there he was, giving in without a struggle.

"But," he added, imperatively, "This won't be a vendetta. You get the job because you're the man for it. But you won't be if you plan to play the Count of Monte Cristo. If you can't tackle the job as if it were just a bunch of goddamn statistics you dug out of a vault somewhere, you'd better let me know about it right now. By the way . . . this man Franks . . . he gets around a little too much for my comfort."

"He's okay," I said. "And he's got a little more guts than he knows. He was ready to cream that guy with an ashtray."

"I checked him out. He seems to have had a very high clearance. He'll have one again if he gets the consultancy he's applied for. I think I might pull a string and get him the job. It has nothing to do with us. It's a liaison in the Executive Office Building. Foreign trade. But you seem to have the key that turns him on, and he doesn't leak information to anybody but you."

"You've been doing some dossier work."

"Just as a matter of course. His contacts—and that crazy orchestra he plays the impresario for—get him into some interesting places. And he knows when to keep quiet."

"That's something," I quipped, "in a nonstop talker like Bob."

"Okay," Hawk said. "I'm going to get him the job. And that'll mean we have ears inside a couple of trade missions who have . . . ." He looked at me sourly. "Who have choked off a lot of useful information lately that might otherwise have wound up in our files."

"All's fair in love and war," I said.

"Nothing's fair in AXE, but I'm not running a den of Cub Scouts. And meanwhile, there's the present business at hand."

"I was wondering when we were going to get back to that," I said.

"Here," he said. He reached under the dash on the right side, pushed—or maybe pulled—something, and a compartment slid down. In it was a file folder. "This is your bedtime story for the evening. It'll bring you far enough up to date for the meeting tomorrow."

"Fine," I said. "What meeting?"

Hawk gnawed on the cigar. It looked like the remains of an old bedroom slipper that had been savaged by a Doberman. "Big Stuff." The words had audible capital letters. "We will have partners in this one. You realize I'm saying this just to cheer you up."

"Damn!"

"Can't be helped. It's international and it busted in our turf. The good people in charge of this are, quite definitely, going to strike again. More than once. That is, unless we can pull a rabbit or two out of a hat in one hell of a hurry."

"Yeah," I sighed. "But . . . ."

"Yes, I know. You prefer playing Paganini fiddle

solos, and it seems like I'm handing you a dull viola part in a Haydn quartet. Well, it won't be quite that way. But you will be working in tandem."

"With how many people?"

"At last count, two." He spat a fragment of mangled tobacco leaf out into the rain.

It was back to anonymous bureaucratic mufti the next day as I walked up the steps to the old Georgetown mansion. There is a way to dress in Washington that makes you look precisely like everybody else in the whole damn town—and that includes Arlington, Alexandria, Silver Spring and Bethesda. At least everybody who works for or with Uncle Sam at a certain level. It's a handy thing to know if you want to disappear utterly. Even the ladies look right through you, even if they'd do a Jerry Lewis double-take if they saw you in T-shirt and jeans; all they can see in that outfit is Executive Paper Shuffler, and they want no part of you. You're not where the action is. You don't control contracts, money, power. Not directly anyhow. The hell with you.

It's a good disguise.

It bought me a snotty sneer from the servant who answered the door. He showed me into a room where I was obviously expected to sit on my ass and wait, and without the usual solace of outdated copies of *National Geographic*. There wasn't the smallest hint of any kind of deference in his manner. Anywhere.

Well, that was Georgetown. They didn't invent the techniques, but they had them down all right.

Sitting there gave me some time to think. I used it to review what I'd learned from Hawk's dossier. It wasn't much. The slug on the front had said: RED SWINEHERD

It seemed that there'd been a recent split-up in the ranks of the Provisional Wing of the Irish Republican Army. The break had been over the recurring dispute between the conservative members and the more fanatical element. The conservatives only wanted to murder every Englishman and every Protestant on the island in their beds, and take over the management of Ulster at gunpoint, enforcing a Catholic rule so repressive and reactionary that even the Vatican frowned on it.

The fanatic element wanted increased terrorist activity, and all the wraps taken off the escalating war. They wanted an assassination a minute. They wanted bombs in hospitals and kindergartens. They wanted tactics that would *really* horrify the British, and not in Whitehall either—in the little constituencies around the country where, in an age that was tired unto the death of bombs and blood, nobody knew what to think any more. Except that, if this was the way they were going to be, let them *have* Ulster, and good riddance.

Of course, the conservative element wanted the same results. But there was a glimmer of common sense in their view of the situation, and it said that after you'd won the war you'd have to be living with your neighbors. And you'd do a bit better with them at the bargaining and trading tables if you hadn't turned their stomachs for good beforehand.

That was the problem, in short. The new group had spun off, in a sanguine snit, from the conservatives who promptly denounced it and read it out of Ireland. The fanatics' reply had been to kidnap a leading Provisional Wing spokesman—an expert incendiary and gunman with a record of thirty personal kills—and torture him to death's door before leaving him, tarred and feathered and nailed to a crude cross, in the middle of a major intersection in downtown Dublin at dawn. He was already in a deep coma when the police found him, and he died before anyone could question him, on a speeding ambulance in the streets of the city by the Liffey.

There hadn't been any doubt about the group that had done this. The nail that had gone through the kidnap victim's right palm had impaled a piece of paper on the way. It read:

> Oh, where's the slave so lowly,
> Condemned to chains unholy,
> Who could he burst
> His bonds accurst,
> Would pine beneath them slowly!

UNION OR DEATH
Rory O'More

The quotation, as it turned out, had been from the poet Thomas Moore, and it had been a favorite of Daniel O'Connell's during the great Repeal fight in 1843, when he had brought a crowd of four hundred thousand to their feet at a mass rally in Mallow by reciting the verse and declaiming afterward, "*I'm* not that slave!"

The pseudonym of the writer went back even farther—to the Tudor days—to a revolt against the English commander of the garrisons in Counties Leix and Offaly, Sir Francis Cosby, who had sequestered the lands of the O'Conors and the O'Mores. The Irish leader in six bloody years of guerrilla warfare had been a boy named Rory O'More. He spelled it, according to records, Ruari Og O'More; but the Irish, in the decline of the Erse tongue, have traditionally used the shorter form. Rory was finally killed in battle—his partisans killed also, some of the children hanged in their mothers' long hair—but the Irish never forgot him. A refrain that still echoed in the country was "God, and Our Lady, and Rory O'More!"

The name of the new organization didn't surface until a week later. It was then that a schoolboy on his way home stumbled across a mutilated body in the streets of Belfast. The body—barely identifiable by now—was naked underneath the tarpaulin in which it had been wrapped. It turned out to be that of Seumas McCarty, a Catholic born and raised, but one of the few voices raised in recent years to ask for conciliation between the warring factions in the Orange Free State. He'd been gutted, castrated, his tongue cut off and his eyelids slit. And then someone had sat him down on the business end of a fine Toledo sword stolen a week earlier from a museum, slowly, letting his weight do the work, until the sword entered his heart. He had bitten through his lips before he died.

Also impaled on the same sword was another verse:

> I shall go to Phelim O'Neill with my
> sorrowful tale, and crave
> A blue-bright blade of Spain, in the ranks
> of soldiers brave.
> And God grant me the strength to
> wield that shining avenger well—
> When the Gael shall sweep his foe
> through the yawning gates of Hell.

UNION OR DEATH
Brian Boy Magee

But this time someone couldn't resist claiming credit for the deed. He called the police station in Belfast and crowed about it. His last words were: *"Beware the Red Swineherd!"*

Everybody knew the references.

"Brian Boy Magee" was the name of a poem by Ethna Carbery—a stirring call to bloody revenge for the punitive action mounted by Scottish troops in 1641, when a Scots force from Carrickfergus drove a band of no less than a thousand Irish women and children over the cliffs on the rocky peninsula called Island Magee.

And the Red Swineherd?

"*A gigantic preternatural figure in Irish Myth,*" said my anonymous, but diligent, compiler of dossiers. "*Where it passes, where it lays its foot, smoke and flames and blood and death and destruction are there. It comes out of some antique past, some dread forgotten ritual . . . .*"

FOUR

"WILL YOU COME in, please?"

The servant who showed me in was the type whom I might be able to impress if I were to flap my arms and fly through the door. As I followed him, I absently stuck my hands in my pockets and fingered a funny, hard rubber object I'd been carrying around for a day or so.

David Hawk nodded at me from a big armchair without getting up. The man behind the desk, however, did get up. He gave me a curt *Mittel-*

Europa nod. He was a burly-looking man with a thick neck and he didn't smile. "Mr. Carter," he said. "I want to talk to you alone . . . ." He turned to Hawk. "In your company, of course, David. Before our two collaborators are shown in I thought it prudent to see you first. Some of what I have to say is for their ears. Some is not." He sat down again. We didn't shake hands.

"Yes, sir," I said. "I understand."

"Then you will perceive the problem here. Beyond the door are agents, working in services much like your own of both the Republic of Ireland and the Irish Free State. We . . ." He noticed my surprise. "Oh, yes," he said. "Both sides. I should perhaps have segregated them while they waited to enter. I don't think they get along with each other."

"I don't understand."

"May I, Mr. Secretary?" Hawk said. He pulled out a cigar and bit into it. He did not light it. The thick-set man leaned back a trifle in his chair and nodded. "Nick. As you can imagine, the activities of the Red Swineherd are not only disturbing in the extreme to the Free State government, they're also profoundly embarrassing to the government of the Republic as well. This time the two governments, convinced of the danger to peace if the present terrorist activities continue have a bounty on the head of any and all members of the organization. In a sense, the agents on the other side of the door are bounty hunters. Their missions are identical and unequivocal: stop the Red Swineherd by any means necessary. There are matters of protocol we can't go into here. At any rate, you're to maintain liaison with them. We've been assured that both of them are excellent agents—tough, resourceful, discreet. I know neither government would send us anyone but their best." He shot lightning bolts at me between well-chosen words. They said: *One outburst and you wind up playing bodyguard for some visiting fireman for a month.*

"Okay," I said. "Sir. Uh . . . but I think you were going to tell me some things first . . . ."

"Right," the man behind the desk broke in. "Of course, we do not want a diplomatic flap. Particularly if your work leads you, as it may, to foreign parts. We have no idea where they will strike next, or at whom. Or where their headquarters is. In short, you are to be discreet . . . ."

"I'm sure he will," Hawk said. "One thing, Nick. The printout we gave you the other day wasn't quite up to date. 'Captain Moonlight' . . . ."

"I was going to ask about him," I said.

"A phrase from a speech by Charles Stewart Parnell," the burly man offered. "After an oration Parnell was asked who would replace him if he were arrested. '*Captain Moonlight,*' said Parnell. He referred to the 'moonlighters'—a popular name for any Irishman willing to strike back at the British, but particularly to strike in stealth, from cover, at night if possible."

"An odd choice of a name for our magician friend," I said, "considering the brassy stunt he pulled off here. Do we have anything on him?"

"Yes," Hawk said in that guttural voice. "He's a real magician as you may have guessed. He is, as Terry said, from Cork, and his name is Daniel O'Grady. He's not the brains of the outfit—that seems to be the one called 'Red Hugh' although that one fact is virtually all we know about their boss. But O'Grady did indeed travel until quite recently as 'The Great Marconi' and he did have a considerable name in Europe, working circuses mostly. Interpol tells us that a few months ago he confided to a friend that he was sick and had only a year to live, and that he was going to go out in style. It seems to have been from that point that he began trying to contact the Red Swineherd organization and offer his considerable services. Well," he continued, "you've seen him, and that's a lead. . . ."

"I'm not completely sure I have," I said. "He was heavily made up. But I did see his eyes. And his ears. Those are identifying areas. Nobody makes up his ears, or tries to cover up their distinctive shape."

"And you've seen his hands . . . ." Hawk said.

"No, sir. I haven't. He wore gloves. He wouldn't even shake hands with me."

"I see. Well, he's a new and dangerous one. You'll have to watch for him. But what we want right now, besides, of course, the destruction of the entire Red Swineherd gang, is the identity of 'Red Hugh.' We're totally stumped, both about that and about their HQ. If only . . . ."

"If only you had a lead?" I said. "Well, I may have something." I reached in my pocket and pulled out the thing I'd been fingering. I put it on the desk.

"What's that?" Hawk said, leaning forward. The man behind the desk picked it up and turned it around in his hands.

"Virtually all that's left of the guy with the dynamite vest Terry Considine chased down the hall. It got thrown my way in the blast, and I picked it up and stuffed it in my pocket at the time. The cops, incidentally, wouldn't like to hear I'd done that."

"Quite all right," the man with the accent said. "Go on."

"Well," I continued, "just for the hell of it I sent it to the lab for a rundown. They informed me that it's just what you thought it was, a rubber heel from his shoe. And that it isn't anything currently in use in shoe repair shops in America, or England, or Canada, or either northern or southern Ireland."

"Hmm." David Hawk scowled at the man behind the desk. "I wonder. Rhodesia, perhaps? South Africa?" He took that pitiful cigar out of his mouth, frowned and dropped it into a wastebasket near his knee. "Have you any ideas, sir?"

The man with the accent looked at him. It wasn't a glare; it just appeared that way because of his thick glasses. Anyone but David Hawk would have shriveled up and died under that heat. "None. Except to say that the people we are talking about have no home or country. They set up housekeeping, always temporarily, in any place where they intend to do business."

"And the business they do in this case is?" I asked.

"Terrorism, pure and simple," the man said flatly. "I should say that when you find out where that piece of rubber comes from, we may have some idea of one of the places where they intend to strike next. Unless of course they have already struck there by then."

"Let's try another tack," I said. "Can you get us up-to-date information on the planned itineraries of all the British ministers, the royal family—anyone who's likely to be a future target?"

Hawk inspected a new cigar. "Already got it, Nick. But that's the problem. These people tend not to kick you on the same shin twice running. That's an angle we have to cover, of course, but it's just as likely to be a hijacking next time. Or what have you."

"Well, that about does it, I guess. Except that I should meet my new friends. I gather they've had the same orientation already."

"Correct," the burly man said. "And . . . well, Mr. Carter, I have explained to David that we deplore the necessity for saddling you with these . . ."

"That's okay, sir," I said. "As long as it's okay for me to give them the shake now and then whenever I need to do some real work."

Hawk's glare grew positively poisonous.

"I understand," the man told me, "but keep up appearances when you can. We actually do need all the help we can get."

"Yes, sir. But there's one thing I don't understand."

"What's that?"

"Our percentage in this?"

"Nick!" Hawk's scolded. He meant it. Lay off.

"No, David, that's all right," the man said. "He's quite right. He should know. Mr. Carter," he said, turning back to me, "three hours ago our Embassy in Ottawa received a note in the mail. It listed several names of officials high in the United States government at the present time. The text said one of these would die within the week. It didn't say which. The note was signed with one of those dreadful poems these people seem to favor, and the pseudonymous identity of the writer was 'Owen Roe'—another hero of the continuing Irish war against the British. And, Mr. Carter, one of the names on the list was my own."

"Oh," I said. I looked at Hawk. He

looked back. He jammed the new cigar back between the molars on the left side of his face. I could see the muscles in his jaw working. "That means here. In D.C. again."

"Or in San Francisco, where I speak before the Bohemian Club tomorrow night. Or in Atlanta, where I address the convention of the Knights of Columbus the night afterward. Or in any one of three other cities I'll visit during the week. Or in any one of a dozen cities where other names on the list have appointments in the next few days."

"And we can't call anyone else in on this. The secretary"—Hawk's head jerked toward our host—"has expressly forbidden that. Which leaves you and me. And our young friends from Ireland."

"We have another problem as well," I said. "They know me."

"Know you? How do you know that?"

"The guy at the Embassy—the one who committed suicide—called me Carter."

The look on Hawk's face said *That's not good. But let's get out of here and compare notes in private.* "Well, we'll deal with that." He turned to the man at the desk, who was getting up. "All right, sir. We'll get right on it."

"Do that, please," the man said. "You will appreciate the personal interest I take in this. Your secretary has, by now, a list of the other names, plus a complete itinerary for all of them. All, even the ones not normally accorded such treatment, have 24-hour Secret Service protection on a high-priority basis from this moment."

"Right, sir." Hawk stood up and I followed suit. The man in the neat gray suit shook hands with us—one little short pump, Central European style, and the smallest sort of bow of the head—and went out.

Hawk looked at me, made a sour face, and shifted the cigar to the other side of his face. "Okay, damn it," he said. "They're over here in the side room. That is, if they haven't blown each other's brains out by now. I suppose we'd better get this over with."

Hawk let me open the door and I followed. The two were sitting on opposite sides of the room, and it was a hell of a big room, but if it had been the Houston Astrodome it would have been too small for the two of them. They stood up when they saw Hawk, though, and something in their manner changed a bit.

"This is Mr. Carter," said Hawk around the cigar. His voice was raspy and sounded irritated under his professional politeness. "He's the agent you'll be working with in this. Nick, this is Miss Sinead Geoghegan of the Republic of Ireland. And Mr. Sean Mulrae of Belfast." I shook hands with each of them and we exchanged greetings.

Sean Mulrae was the one who looked Irish. He was redheaded and round-faced and had the same green eyes you'd expect if you'd sent out to Central Casting. His grip was strong as a gorilla's, and made you take another look at him with, perhaps, an eyebrow raised. He simply didn't look hefty enough—he was perhaps five-feet-eight, and might come in at a hundred fifty—to have that kind of fist on him. His eye was clear and looked as though, in other circumstances, there might have been a gleam of humor in it.

Sinead Geoghegan was what they called a "black Irish." The hair was bright, glossy, gleamy black, squeaky clean, and had a fetching wave in it at shoulder length. The skin was Byronically pale. The eyes were dark, with bright flashes in them. She was mad as hell about something, and I was glad it wasn't at me. She wore a tweed skirt and a bulky Irish sweater, and the body that showed through was the kind that takes your breath away. She'd have looked sexy and half-dressed in a diving suit.

She pressed my hand warmly—and her grip wasn't as strong as his, but it had a lot of muscle behind it in its own way.

"I . . . you'll have to forgive us, please,"

she said, trying to smile through the rage that was running through her. "We . . . we've been after having a bit of a row."

"Damned right, too," Sean muttered, stuffing his hands into capacious pockets of his Irish-cut suit. "Bloody papist bitch."

"You dare!" she said in a voice suddenly gone huffy. "You pro-British . . . you quisling, you. . . ."

I stepped back and looked at Hawk. His brows were furrowed and his expression full of disbelief. It was going to be a hell of a week!

FIVE

"WE DO HAVE something of a dossier on this O'Grady, but . . ." Hawk was talking as he tried to find a parking place on Massachusetts Avenue near Dupont Circle.

It had taken several minutes and quite a bit of diplomacy to calm down our two collaborators and get them out to the car. I never did find out what their heated argument was about; it didn't matter, it seems it was only a preliminary bout.

"Oh, yes, sir." Sean Mulrae offered enthusiastically. "I'm having our files on him sent to you. We've quite a bit of information. Odd, though, that the bloody bastard should choose a knife this time. With a knife in the chest you have to face your victim. O'Grady will usually stick with something nice and safe, like plastic bombs on a postbox, where even a schoolchild can set it off and lose an arm."

Sinead Geoghegan was in a huff now, the anger showing hot in her eyes. "Coward he may be, and murderer, but our own dossier on the man includes devil a word about him raping or tarring and feathering innocent Catholic convent girls in the streets of Londonderry like—"

"Oh, if it's atrocities we'll be talking about," Sean cut her off," we could always mention . . . ."

Hawk exchanged a knowing glance with me and spoke above both their voices. "Nick, Bialek's has a book I ordered a month ago. I think I'll drop by and pick it up. You can take Sean and Sinead upstairs, and I'll meet you there in about twenty minutes."

"Oh, sure," I said through gritted teeth. "And *thanks*!" I stared at him before he pulled away. He caught my look and knew that he owed me one.

"But if your people hadn't . . ." It was Sinead.

"And for the love of Jesus, why shouldn't they?" Sean countered.

For Christ's sake, they were still bickering. They didn't even notice that Hawk had left. I tried to interrupt, but they were really at it this time.

"Oh, sure to God you're not going to bring up that poppycock about Bango and Ballymena," Sinead was saying. "British propaganda even a child could see through in a moment . . ."

"I do beg your pardon," said Sean sarcastically. "I've only just got through having a look at eight by ten glossy photographs by the dozen: mangled bodies, women, children . . ."

"Oh, and splendid photos they are too," Sinead said angrily. "They were made in a film studio in Yugoslavia, using the finest modern techniques—"

I'd had enough. "For the love of God, you two." I almost screeched the words, so that Sinead stopped talking in midsentence and they both turned to glare at me. I realized then that I handled the situation unwisely. Calming down, I said to Sean, "There's a cafeteria on the ground floor. Would you mind bringing up four coffees? It's Room Number—"

"Oh, I know the room," Sean said. "I'll be glad to bring them; be right up."

I didn't bother to speculate as to how the hell he knew which room. I sure hadn't told him, and neither had David, and I'd have put money on the notion that the secretary hadn't told him before he ducked out. All I knew was that AXE would probably have another damned faceless office within a couples of days. Hawk had a thing about people knowing where he was. He didn't like it! I'm not talking about the front—Amalgamated Press—

but the real office, the one with the files.

Now, however, the atmosphere changed appreciably, and as we waited for the elevator I turned around and got another look at Sinead Geoghegan.

The flush in her cheeks, red as rouge on her pale skin, was attractive as all hell. And she knew she was attractive; women, no matter how young, have an infallible instinct about such things.

"I'm sorry," she said. "I . . . it's an all but insoluble problem we have, and it's a blessed small island to be locked up in with it. You have to understand the provocations come daily, sometimes oftener . . . ."

"Yeah," I said. I looked at the dark eyes and the full lips curving in an ironic smile. There was a lot of intelligence in her look, and no coquetry at all. That suited me just fine. I like a woman who looks you in the eye and makes up her own mind. And she had a kind of natural grace that made everything she did look sexy.

Well, everything she did when she was out of earshot from Sean Mulrae, anyhow.

I sighed and opened the elevator door.

We were barely inside when I felt something wrong. And the minute the elevator started I *knew* something was wrong.

It was an old elevator—an Otis, with the old-fashioned fancy logo mounted on several sides. It reminded me of David Hawk's car; old and cranky, but serviceable.

Now, all of a sudden, it began jerking its way

upward in wild lurches. One of them sent Sinead to her knees and damn near knocked me over too.

It passed our floor and kept going. Seven, eight, nine. I hit the emergency button but nothing happened. I grabbed at the door. Usually if you can get the door open a bit it'll jam the car and stop it. Now the damn thing wouldn't give. "Here," I said. "Give me a hand. Get your fingers in here . . . now when I say heave . . . ."

We pulled hard and the car shuddered to a stop.

We were stuck between floors. You could see about six inches of the door above and below us. There wasn't room to crawl through even if you could get the door open.

I took one very tentative step toward the middle of the car.

The car shivered, the motor growled, the car dropped four inches.

I looked at Sinead Geoghegan. Her eyes were excited, her face still wearing that fetching flush. It wasn't fear, whatever else it may have been. I had to give her that.

"Maybe," I said, "I could give you a leg up and you could get through the door."

"I don't think so," she said. "It'll take time to pry the door open. I don't think we have that kind of time. The lift's ready to fall."

"I think you're right. Okay. The only way out is through the roof. Come here." She slipped out of her sensible Irish shoes and put one stockinged foot in my cupped hands. When she stepped up those nice legs nestled against my cheeks—and the car dropped another six inches.

"These lifts," she said, "usually have a door. Yes, here . . . . I think I can lift it out of the way . . ."

The car shook like a six-point earthquake. I damn near dropped her.

"Ah, yes," she said. "That's the brake. It's old and it's slipping. And . . . oh, Jesus, Mary and Joseph. You should see the dinky strand of cable that's holding this thing up. It's been cut through, Nick. Cut right down to one strand . . . ."

"Yeah," I said. "All the more reason to get the hell out of here."

She got the picture and crawled up and through that little door with a lot less fuss than I would have done considering that broken and slipping brake. She was agile and strong and moved like a cat.

In a moment she was up on top of the car looking down at me through the little door. "Here, Nick," she said. "Take my hand . . . ."

"I can get out by myself," I said. "Sinead, for the love of God get the hell out of here. You ought to be able to reach the door from there. Get through it. Damn it, go . . . ."

As if to underline what I was saying, the car took another sickening lurch. It dropped a foot this time.

"Nick," she said. Her voice had an edge on it. "Come along. The shoe on that brake . . . ."

I took that pretty hand she was holding out to

me, intending just to use it to steady myself as I climbed up. Instead she pulled hard and steady, and lifted me off my feet.

"Okay," I said when I had both hands on the sill. "I've got it. Now clear out." She backed off, but stood ready to give me a hand.

The car slipped, slowly, down another inch or so. There was a smell of scorched rubber from that badly frayed brake shoe. As I climbed I could see the cable above me. And that single strand they'd left uncut was unwinding at the edges . . . slowly. . . .

I slipped through the door and sat on the car. It took another ghastly lurch. She tottered, but held on. "All right," she said. "I tried the door a moment ago. I can't move it. You'll have to do it for me."

"Okay." I stepped past her. Damned if she didn't smile at me. It was a mildly worried smile, but it was a good Irish smile nonetheless. She had a bit of sand in her, no doubt about that. "Hey, damn it," I said. "Why don't you get up on that crossbeam?" I gestured at a big "I" beam. "And get behind the beam, too. When that last strand pops the cable's going to lash around like blue blazes. You don't want it to catch you and knock you off."

"Nick, if it breaks . . . for God's sake get the door open. You're still standing on the car, remember?"

How could I forget? But there wasn't anyplace

else to stand while I clawed at that goddamned door. It didn't want to move; for a moment I thought I had it, and then the brake squealed, and the motor roared, and the car dropped another four inches.

The next time the thing slipped it would either go just far enough to keep me from being able to reach the door . . . or it would drop me ten floors into the basement.

I threw caution to the winds and heaved.

The door opened . . . just a crack . . . then a little more . . . The car beneath me shuddered and threatened. I could feel it give, little by little. I looked up and watched tiny flecks of rubber fly from the brake as it dragged precariously at the rail.

I yanked at the door again and the car fell out from underneath me completely.

As I started to fall I got one hand on the door, good and solid. Straining for it saved my life. By ducking I kept the broken end of the cable, flailing about like crazy, from taking my head off. Even so, the single strand—the one that hadn't wanted to give—lashed past me and neatly slit my coat right up the back without even touching the shirt I wore underneath.

Hanging by one hand, I watched the elevator below me get smaller and smaller . . . and land with a crash that was deafening in the echoing shaft.

I swung around, facing the wall again, and reached desperately up for that door. And as I did the first hand lost a little more purchase. My legs dangled aimlessly . . . my other hand was slipping.

I looked up. Sinead stood inside the door. She was ripping her stocking off, peeling it off her leg. As I watched, she braced herself, both hands on the rail outside in the corridor, and reached one bare foot and ankle down for me to grab. "Hurry," she said. "Your hand would slip on nylons. Here, grab hold, Nick. Quick!"

I grabbed.

First one hand, then the other. She braced herself and gave another tug, again surprisingly strong. She held on to that railing with an iron grip and backed one millimeter at a time into the corridor, dragging my 180-pound weight behind her.

She backed against the wall, looking at me. Her eyes closed for a long blink, and opened again to look at me some more. "Jesus, Mary and Joseph," she said. She was all relieved tension for a moment, then she looked around her, getting her bearings. "My God," she said. "That should have waked the dead. And there's not a person at all in the hall here. Hasn't anyone any curiosity here?"

"Sorry about that," I said. "That's the kind of building this is. Hey, you looked pretty good in there, pal," I said.

"Ah, God," she said. Her face was drawn. "I'm usually all right while these things are happening. It . . . it's afterward that I'm a coward." She was blushing and it looked nice as hell on that pale skin. To cover her embarrassment she pulled off the other stocking. "I . . . I suppose that's it for my shoes," she said.

"Don't worry," I said, getting up. "This is Dupont Circle, after all. Nobody wears shoes around Dupont Circle. I'll tell everybody you're in training to be a hippie."

That drew one of those nice smiles. "I . . . I've got another pair at the apartment," she said lamely.

"Come on," I said. "Forget about that. We've got to get downstairs . . . ."

I didn't finish the sentence. *"Nick!"* a familiar voice bellowed. I wheeled and went back to the shaft and looked down. Four floors below David Hawk, standing in the sixth floor, stared up the shaft at me. "What the hell is going on? Is Miss. . . ."

"Yeah," I said. "This Irish ladyfriend of yours saved my neck. Hang on. We'll be right down. And David. Don't touch your door until I get there."

It took us a whole minute and a half to make it there. Well, maybe two minutes. I bounced down the stairs two and three at a time, Sinead close behind me, silent on her bare feet.

When we got to the sixth-floor landing we ran into Sean Mulrae. "What the devil?" he said. "The lift . . . it isn't working . . . ." He held a cardboard box bearing four coffees. His expression was puzzled, but his eye on us was sharp and took everything in—her bare feet, my filthy suit and slashed coat, the grease all over both of us. "Something's happened," he said.

"Brilliant," the girl said.

"Don't either one of you start anything." I said. "Come along." I shoved the door open to face David Hawk. He was standing there waiting for an explanation. His glare wouldn't settle for anything half-baked.

"What's this about my door?" he said.

"I meant it. Don't touch it until I've had a look. I know you know about these things. I know you can give me lessons any day in the week in demolition-squad techniques. But I'm not taking any chances." I looked at him. "You *know* what I'm talking about."

"Oh?" he said. He reached for a cigar.

"I didn't see that list of names in the secretary's office," I said, "and you did. But I know that that cable was cut. And I know . . . ."

"Then you know," Hawk said, "that one of the names on the list was my own."

SIX

"AH," SAID SEAN Mulrae. Then he did a sort of double take as the implications hit him. "Ah, now. That *is* unfortunate, isn't it? Complicates things terribly." His sharp young eye caught mine, and a wry expression twisted one side of his mouth.

"I don't understand," Sinead said. "What list?"

"The list the secretary got in the mail not five hours ago. In Ottawa. The one he didn't tell us about in the interview."

"Oh?" I said. "Tell me more." I folded my arms over my chest and looked at him with new eyes. "If he didn't tell you about it I'm a little curious as to how you . . . ."

"Come inside," Hawk said. He took a hard look at the door and opened it as if I hadn't warned him. "Don't worry, Nick. I've got that door bugged. If anybody messes with it while I'm out I can tell."

"I should have known." We went in. Hawk sat down and pointed the three of us at chairs. Sean, shutting the door behind him, looked both ways in the hall first. "Now, Mr. Mulrae. You were saying."

"Oh, yes. The list was delivered to your Embassy in Canada. It wasn't exactly Foreign Papers Please Copy, and it wasn't routinely released to Reuters, but we have a way of hearing about these things fairly quickly."

"You sure as hell do." I dug out one of my monogrammed smokes and looked at it. I can't make up my mind whether or not to quit smoking. Maybe I don't want to. Every time the tailormades run out I reorder as a matter of course. "Go on."

"Yes," Sinead said. "And it would help if you'd be getting to the point."

"And of course I made a quick phone call while I was out getting cof—God almighty, I forgot the coffee. Here. They're all black. There's cream and sugar if anyone wants. Saccharine," he said with a quick glance at Sinead's tweedy, but trim, bottom, "for any of us as is on a diet at the moment." The glance she shot back at him would have killed anyone but an Irishman. "Now," he said, ignoring her, "our people tell me the list contains several names of interest. And it stands to reason, doesn't it, that if all these names are of people marked for death . . . ."

"Please," said Sinead impatiently, "get to the point."

"Exactly," he said. "And if one of the names your dear friend 'Owen Roe' intends to murder during the coming week . . . ."

"He's no friend of mine," she snapped.

"You couldn't prove it by me. But as I say, if one of them was Mr. Hawk here . . . why, that means a serious compromise of security in your agency, doesn't it? And that means . . . ah, Christ, we might as well all wear name tags, and take out ads telling where we are and what we're doing . . . ."

"*Yes?*" Hawk cut in, glaring at young Mulrae. "And I'm sure you have some alternative suggestions?"

Mulrae looked at Hawk; caught that ice-cold eye of his for a moment; and blinked. "Ah . . . sorry, sir. I didn't mean to be flip. It's just that this changes the situation a bit, now, doesn't it? I mean . . . if AXE's security has been blown . . . ."

"Nick," Hawk said. I took my cue. I was out of the chair in a second and I jumped him. He got one arm between my fist and his jaw, but it didn't do much more than deflect a blow that would have taken his head off if it had landed squarely. As it was it spun him over the back of his chair, scattering hot coffee every which way.

He was strong and agile. He spun in the air and landed with his feet under him. He reached for his coat pocket, but stopped. Wilhelmina was out and cocked, her twin sights zeroing in on his chest before he could move another muscle.

"Okay," I said. "Spread-eagle against the wall. Support yourself with your fingertips, feet about four feet back. The Luger is going in your ear. One false move while Miss Geoghegan pats you down and cleans out your pockets and believe me, buster, you've got yourself a problem."

"Mind telling me . . ." he asked, "what all this is about?" His voice was a little strained. There was blood running down his jaw from a split lip.

"Just taking no chances," Hawk said, watching Sinead pat him down expertly and remove a private arsenal before dumping the other contents of his pockets on the floor. "I have only the secretary's word that you're Sean Mulrae. And you were the only person besides myself who wasn't on that elevator when it went down. And you know too goddamn much." He bent over and picked up the wallet. He looked over wallet and papers; grunted. "Nick. See if he's got a scar on the outside of the right calf, size of a quarter; deep; white scar tissue."

"Yeah," I said, checking, "it's real. And it's not new from the look of it."

"Okay. Let him up." He watched as Mulrae got

to his feet, looking hard at all of us. Not mad, hard. Appraising us. "Sorry," Hawk told him, but his tone wasn't apologetic. "You know the rules of the game."

"Sure," Mulrae said. "Sure I do. And I—I suppose I'd have done the same." He looked at me and wiggled his jaw, testing it. "Jesus Christ," he said. "You throw a mean punch." He shook his head and grinned that Irish grin. Heredity doesn't ask you which side of the border you come from.

"However," Hawk said, "the problem you brought up remains a problem. It's true. I'll have to move. We're on red alert within AXE from this moment. That's all you two," he nodded at Sean and Sinead, "need to know. Except that looking out for me is not part of your job. Nor yours, Nick. Your job is to stop these people. Now sit down here, all of you. The secretary had to leave before he could finish his orientation. I'll finish the job right now. If you have anything to add to what we know, don't keep it to yourselves."

We broke up an hour later. David had dropped a hint to me in the conversation to call in at nine using the "B" Code phone number. Nobody but me seemed to have caught it. He showed us out. I knew that shortly the Amalgamated Press and Wire Services would be on their way to temporary relocation in the National Press Building and David Hawk's office would be as vacant as if it had never been occupied at all.

Sean Mulrae gave us a jaunty grin and begged off when I invited the two of them to dinner. He'd see us in the morning, he said; we were to get together at the AXE lab in McLean and have a look at the analysis of the damned little our bomber friends had left to trace them by. As he turned to leave he flexed his jaw again, using one hand. "Christ," he said, "some right hand there . . ." And he went out.

I turned to Sinead. "You're not going to turn me down too? I kind of owe you a meal. I don't know whether that pays you back for my still having a whole skin, but . . . ."

She smiled up at me with those dark eyes. "I'd love to go to dinner with you, Nick."

We caught a cab and went down to Chez François. It's not as tony as the Rive Gauche, and you'll never run into Jackie Onassis or Walter Cronkite there, but it's a lot more real for my dough.

We stopped at Sinead's hotel room on the way to get her shoes and let her change. I thought about my ripped coat, my dirty face . . . and for a moment I thought of going back to my apartment to change. Then I said the hell with it, and when she was done with the bathroom I went in to wash up. The coat I stuffed down the garbage disposal after I'd removed all my valuables. I stowed Wilhelmina's little holster inside my shirt and borrowed a scarf from Sinead to improvise myself an ascot. Chez François isn't all that snooty about dress.

She was quiet and subdued during the cab ride and throughout most of the meal. I tried to get her talking several times, but she was unresponsive. She ate her Chateaubriand with a surprising heartiness, though, considering her trim frame and thin bones.

Finally she looked up and said, "My God. I can't eat another bite." Smiling, she pushed the plate away. "Nick, it was marvelous. And . . ." she put her hand on mine "thanks ever so much for putting up with me. I—I don't know how to explain it. I just didn't feel like talking."

"Happens," I said. I picked up the bottle of wine and poured the dark red liquid into her glass. "Don't think any more of it."

"No," she said. The hand tightened on mine. "I—I must explain. I mean, why I was so terrible about Mulrae today. I mean . . . ."

"Terrible?" I shook my head and took a drink. "No. Edgy, maybe, I understand things are bad over there."

"No, it's not just that." Her mouth trembled, just once, and the dark eyes dipped to the tablecloth. Then she was under control again. "Nick, I—I'm not *Miss* Geoghegan. I was 'Miss" MacManus . . . oh, a year ago. But I married another agent in our service, Hugh Geoghegan. He was a handsome young widower, oh, I'd guess about your age . . . ."

"You can't imagine how I like the juxtaposition of 'young' and 'your age'," I said.

"Ah, right," she said, smiling—but the smile was a thing that turned dark and bitter in spite of her. "I—I was saying . . . Hugh had two children from his first marriage, a boy and a girl, seven and five years old. Lovely children, both of them, and a month after the marriage I already had begun to think of them as my own. I loved them, I . . . ." Here she faltered a bit, and I could see tears glinting in the dark eyes by the soft candlelight. "Nick. O'Grady. He played a benefit performance, in that 'Marconi' getup of his, at a street fair in Dublin. Hugh was well known to the Red Swineherd organization as a man who was after them. We weren't on to O'Grady then. And he came into the audience at the end, and picked our . . . our children . . . to help him demonstrate his act . . ."

"Sinead," I said. I put my other hand on hers.

"And—and he was supposed to leave this empty opera hat on the edge of the stage . . . and to show he had nothing to do with it, he'd back away, away off into the wings . . . and little Seamus was to reach inside, and there'd be a rabbit or whatever. And Hugh edged closer with little Brigid in his—his arms, and . . . ."

"Hey," I said. "Here."

She was sobbing now, very quietly, as if her heartbreak could never be cured. "Nick . . . the bomb went off . . . thirty children killed . . . sixteen more injured . . . and all my three . . . Hugh and the babies . . . the only people I had left to care for in all the world . . . ."

"Jesus," I said. I wanted to say something like yeah, honey, I know how you feel. But I didn't. All

I could say was, "Sinead." It's a pretty name: Shin-*aid;* it's the Erse equivalent of Jane. I squeezed her hand and she squeezed me back, hard.

Presently she put herself back together, and it was impressive watching her. She was tough as nails, for all her youth. What was she? Twenty-five? Twenty-six? She smiled up at me, and it didn't turn bitter this time. It just kind of clouded over a bit. "I . . . thanks, Nick. I think I will be able to deal with it, you know. But it's only been a month."

"Jesus." I put on my hearty front. "A month? Geoghegan, you're tough as they come. I'd still be unstuck."

"The devil you would. But thanks, Nick. And . . . I told them, anyhow, that if they didn't give me this one that was all. And they must have decided that it was better to use me than to lose me. I'm going to catch O'Grady, and he's coming to a justice he's never dreamed of." Her dark eyes had flinty streaks in them in the light.

"*We're* going to catch O'Grady," I said.

"All right . . . but he's not going to spend five years in some cushy jail living the life of Reilly. He's going to pay, in the poor currency of his life, for . . . ."

I looked at her hard. And nodded. I remembered Terry Considine.

When I dropped her at her door at eight-fifteen that dark smile came up at me with a wave of warmth, she pressed my hand, and started to go inside . . . and then the next thing I knew she was in my arms with a sob and kissing me hard, those strong little arms around my neck, those fine breasts pressed hard against me. I could feel her heart pounding . . . . Chemistry might well have taken over. But a month? It was too soon. She didn't have her feelings all sorted out yet.

Suddenly she slipped in the door and shut it after her without another word.

I shrugged and walked away, out to the cab. I had a lot to think about as I rode through the dark streets of the city . . . .

David Hawk on the list! And how had they got through to us—how did they know Hawk's name, and the address of AXE, and Hawk's schedule? Because, damn it, that had been precisely timed. To be sure, it was one of those thousand government holidays Washington has, which left fairly sparse traffic in a building like ours, with its network of lobbyists' offices and minor government-bureau offices and the sort of hangers-on who free-lance editing, and art, and clerical services to them. But how could they count on Hawk and his party being the first people to come along after they sawed through every strand in that elevator cable but one? Without knowing his precise schedule?

One thing was sure. If Hawk hadn't gotten irritated by Sean and Sinead and their bickering—and I thought I might take a more tolerant attitude toward it myself now, knowing what I knew—and stepped down to Bialek's bookstore on Connecticut for a moment, all three of us would be dead. Because that cable wouldn't have held three people long enough to let us get out, the way it had held two. No way . . . .

I took the elevator up to my place, thinking about all this, and I was still a bit preoccupied when I reached my door.

My hand went to the doorhandle . . . and stopped. I held it there in the air, almost unwilling to move it backward or forward. I stepped back a step. There it was again. That goddamned sixth-sense business.

Now, looking around, I remembered the transom hook at the end of the hall. I went for it and brought it back, walking very softly. Sticking back close to the wall, I gingerly reached out and tried jiggling the doorhandle to my apartment . . . .

The blast knocked me for a loop. It blew holes in my wall, and in my absent neighbor's—he sells pianos—and in the wall opposite me. When I got up I felt as if somebody'd just shot off a howitzer a couple of inches from my ear, and I had to shake my head to stop the ringing.

Then, as I got up and brushed myself off, I shook it again. It was still ringing.

I went to the door of what had been my apartment.

The phone ringing inside.

I walked over to it—amazingly, it was nearly the only thing in the room that wasn't destroyed—and picked it up.

"Hello, Nick," a familiar voice said. "Hawk here . . . ."

SEVEN

I LOOKED OVER in the corner where my bed had been. Like everything else in the room it was a godawful mess, and now, as I watched, I could see it smolder and burst into flame.

"Nick!" the voice said. "You there?"

"Hello, sir," I said. "Somebody just blew my apartment to hell. Somehow the phone seems to have been immune. I'm not sure what they used. If it was a plastic bomb it was a hell of a big one. Had I been here, there wouldn't be anything left of me to identify.

"Just happened, you say?" Hawk's voice had a curious tension in it.

"The phone rang about the same time it happened. I thought I triggered it with the transom hook; I had a hunch and wasn't taking any chances. But I don't know. Could the phone itself have triggered it?"

"Don't worry about that. Is there a side entrance? Something private?"

"Yeah. Hell, you know that. You were up here playing poker with me and Considine not a month ago."

"Well, slip out of it and get away quick. Don't take anything with you. Don't let anybody see you leaving. When you're about six blocks away grab a pay phone and call me. And if you have anything on you—not in the room, on you—that would do as a disguise, use it."

"I don't understand."

"Don't try. Get out of there and call me. As of right now, you're dead. That bomb blew you to hell."

"Huh?" I said. But he'd hung up. And I knew better than to stick around and puzzle it out. For some reason Hawk wanted it to look as though the bomb had got me, and I wasn't supposed to wait around and react. I slipped out the side entrance and took off. And not a damned moment too soon. You could hear the sirens in the distance already.

I looked up and down the alley, then cut across and ducked into somebody's garden a moment to pull out my wallet. Inside was a shaggy student-type moustache, with a little dab of spirit gum on it. I worked it into place, then pulled the edges down over the corners of my mouth. I was wearing my hair a little longer and shaggier than usual and this made it fairly easy to comb it forward until it covered my ears. Then I dumped the ascot, stowing it behind a busted brick in an adjacent wall. I rolled up my sleeves, slightly above the elbow, and opened the collar another button. Then, I yanked a couple of ballpoints out of my pocket and stuck them in my shirt pocket. An aging teaching assistant from G.W. University. Getting a little long in the tooth, but still no tenure.

I slipped around the house and moved to the rear of the crowd that had already gathered. I asked a few dumb questions, the way people do. Then, as the cop cars pulled up—they were one block ahead of the fire trucks—I slowly walked away, attracting no attention at all.

I kept up the unhurried pace for two blocks in one direction, two blocks in another. Then I cut down an alley and strolled along one of the diagonal boulevards for a block before turning forty-five degrees into a cross street.

I called Hawk.

"Nick?" he said. He hadn't even let the phone ring twice. "You got away okay?"

"So far so good. What's up?"

"I got on the hot line. There'll be a guy with the coroner's office there who will find traces of you.

He'll certify you dead. The cops will know better, but they also know when to clam up."

"Go on." I didn't like the light in the booth, shining on my face. What the hell, it was an all but deserted street, but it didn't pay to take any chances. I reached up and turned it off.

"You'll have figured out by now that another of the names on that list was your own," Hawk said. "This time they got you. There will be a notice in the *Post* and the *Star*. There'll be a burial service, just like Terry's, small and private. And in the meantime I'll be going underground. I'm going after the D.C. chapter of this organization myself."

"And the late Nick Carter?" I asked.

"You're taking off for Atlanta. There's a private eye named Lou Russell there—a black guy, very smart and sharp—who has a couple of tips to share with us. He can't leave because he's got somebody staked out who may be the one they call 'Rory O'More.' I want you to join him and see what you can find out. Before you eliminate 'Mr. O'More,' that is."

"Okay. Piece of cake. Go on. Obviously you've thought this out and you have a whole shopping list for me."

"Right. Then there's a contact in London. Remember the affair in Bulawayo, back before Rhodesia declared independence?"

"Oh, yeah. The British First Secretary for. . . ."

"Right. He'll have a Whitehall number. Call it.

He'll clue you in. Get on that the minute you leave Atlanta. Big stuff. If the Atlanta thing didn't look so promising I'd send you to London tonight. But the world's a powder keg now, and I can't spare anybody to spell you. The contact in London is in the cabinet now, all these years later. He'll get you in anywhere you need to go. There's trouble brewing there, and perhaps in Amsterdam. I still can't figure out why we can't get a positive ID on that boot heel. Dick McDougal in the lab says it's got him stumped. But maybe I'll have something for you by the time you get to London. You can always get me on Hot Line Five."

"What about those two kids assigned to me? Are they being clued in on the matter?"

"Assigned to whom? A dead man?"

"Okay, I wasn't looking forward to dragging them around, sharp as they are. Although the Geoghegan girl. . . ."

"Forget it." Hawk said emphatically. "You're dead. Now get cracking, or it'll be both our funerals. Take a cab to Baltimore. You're leaving from there; I'm not taking any chances of having you seen at National or Dulles. When you get to Friendship ask at the checkstand for a package for Mr. Bender . . . you do have your 'Mr. Bender' IDs?"

"Yes, sir. Fortunately, I didn't leave 'em in the apartment." I looked around. The streets were empty. Washington changes more radically from block to block than anywhere. Six blocks from my middle-class neighborhood, here I was in an area where half the buildings were condemned—some of them had been ever since the '68 riots—and yet nobody could get the dough to demolish them, much less to build on the ground.

"You'll need clothes. Charge them at Rich's in Atlanta. You won't be able to look up Lou Russell until tomorrow anyhow. The package for Bender will have a ticket on tonight's flight, some dough, and some info. Use the codebook. You didn't lose that in the fire, did you?"

"I never leave anything like that in the house."

"Okay. Some nice light reading on the plane, then, or at your hotel. There'll be more info waiting for you in London. That's it for now, Nick. Your plane leaves at midnight."

"I'm gone," I said, and hung up.

It was interesting to be dead and if I had anything to say about it I was sure going to scare the hell out of a few people. I hoped Hawk would have the presence of mind to save the obits for me. They'd be one-paragraph items, buried in the great featureless middles of those bulky D.C. papers. People in AXE don't make the front pages. But I wanted them anyway for the john wall of my next apartment . . . .

When the plane took off from Friendship Airport I was on it, sitting alone by a window, my "Mr. Bender" package in my hand. I looked around; the plane was half empty.

"Mr. Bender" was a useful alter ego to be letting loose on the world, right now. Because there was something about him that nobody took seriously at first.

There is a kind of rich guy who comes on like a slob. He looks like an unmade bed. He sometimes shaves, sometimes doesn't. You take one look at him, with his dumb chino pants and frayed and scuffed chukka boots and his hair going every which way, and you dismiss him. Waiters ignore him at restaurants, to seat the distinguished-looking gentleman with the Brooks Brothers suit and the silver-gray hair. Usually the distinguished one passes bum credit cards and the hobo type with the five o'clock shadow could buy and sell Howard Hughes.

This was "Mr. Bender." He could disappear into the wallpaper virtually anywhere in the world, from the Bath and Tennis Club in Palm Beach to a Skid Row flophouse in Seattle. It was only when you started to check out his credit that you found he was A-Okay with every bank from continent to continent.

Right now, as "Mr. Bender" I was occupying a whole quarter of a 707 all by myself, and couldn't ask for a better chance to catch up on my reading. I dug out the codebook and went to work, after looking around to make sure the stewardess was otherwise occupied. She was.

Now, though, the codebook and the encrypted

info Hawk had passed along to me turned out to be interesting reading. It appeared that a lot of what he'd told me in front of Sean and Sinead had been strictly speaking for Buncombe. Apparently he knew the names of those who'd have attempts made on their lives. And where. And when.

That morning—too late for it to be in the secretary's orientation—AXE Agent N15, Wally Burger, had nabbed a Red Swineherd man in Portland, Oregon, just as he'd prepared to board a plane for Anchorage. Wally had taken him down to a basement below a poolroom and . . . well, Wally didn't have much time, and asking *pretty please* would in the best of times have been counterproductive. It took the terrorist a whole hour to break and spill his guts. Then, the moment Wally had eased up on him a bit, he self-destructed. Using a razor blade that was tucked into a little pocket inside his shirt collar, he'd carved himself a brand new smile about five inches below the old one, from ear to ear. . . .

But the information had been there. And Hawk had it now.

It hadn't included any names. Apparently the members of the group only knew members of their own cell. Damn Robert A. Heinlein, anyhow. In one of his science fiction novels he'd outlined a perfect structure for a terrorist organization—and we'd been running into variants of his structure ever since.

What it had included, now, was quite enough to

occupy me to my heart's content for a week or two.

The main things were these:

Nick Carter was to die today. (Well, he had. No . . . I looked at my watch now . . . it was yesterday by now. R.I.P.)

David Hawk was to die tomorrow, in Washington. (No, that was today. Well, hang in there, Hawk. If you can't take care of yourself after forty years in the service and hundreds of similar attempts, well . . .)

The third attempt . . . that was why I was going to Atlanta. That was why Russell was already at work. There was the formal dinner of the Knights of Columbus convention at the big Exhibition Hall out on Forrest and the speaker was going to get it, right in the middle of his speech. In front of six thousand people. On a national television hookup. On prime time.

And who was he?

Who else but the man with the thick glasses and the *Mittel-Europa* accent, the man who had called David Hawk and me in this morning to lay out our chores for us.

EIGHT

THE HOTEL PEOPLE got me out of bed at eight. There was complimentary coffee and Continental breakfast if I wanted it, delivered to my room. I settled for coffee. I wasn't going to go all the way to Georgia and miss out on a real honest-to-God Southern breakfast, even if it meant getting started a little later in the day than usual.

There was a bit of business to be dealt with first. I reached for the central Atlanta phone book, found a number, and dialed.

"Louis Russell Enterprises," the voice on the other end said. "Russell speakin'."

"Lou? Nick Carter."

"Oh, *yeah.*" The voice sounded more interested already. "That was quick."

"You've got some information for me, I think. And . . ."

"Where are you?"

"Greenbrier Hotel. I'm about to go downstairs and make the acquaintance of easy-overs, grits, country ham with red-eye gravy, and biscuits. . . ."

"Well, you ain't gonna find 'em at the Greenbrier. It's been bought by a chain and now everything's all Fast Food. Look, I'll be down to pick you up. I'll be drivin' a taxi of the Golden Boy Cab Co., of which I have the honor to be president, sole driver, and exalted panjandrum. Fifteen minutes in front of the hotel?"

"Make it a half hour in front of Rich's. I have to buy some emergency threads off the rack in a hurry. Somebody blew up my apartment last night."

"Oh, yeahhhhh . . . ." It was the equivalent of a long low whistle. "I see the other side don't waste any time. Well, it's nice to be dealin' with professionals for a change. Half hour? Rich's? Right on, man . . . ."

I was standing there trying to get the off-the-rack coat to stop binding in the shoulders when the Golden Boy cab pulled up. It was a big flashy Mercury Monterey about ten years old, and the power plant inside it sounded like it ought to be running a yacht.

Russell's face, chocolate-brown, round and cheery, appeared at the window. "Nick? Get in, man. I'm hungry," he said opening the back door. I slammed it and got in beside him in the front seat instead. He shot me a modified soul handshake and put the big car in gear. "Them Howard Johnson-style breakfasts is for the tourists, man," he said, cornering expertly as he accelerated. "Now I know this little place over here on Peachtree . . . ."

"Peachtree? I thought the Greenbrier was on Peachtree."

"Peachtree Street, Northwest," Russell said with an amiable grin. "Not to be confused with Peachtree Street Northeast. Or with any of the approximately 26 other streets, lanes, boulevards, alleys, and avenues bearing the name of Peachtree within a mile or two of Five Points. Sometimes folks find it's so confusin' findin' their way around they hire a private detective like just to locate an address. And then the drivin' turns out to be so much of a pain they gotta hire me to take 'em there. Any town that helps the independent small businessman along like that is okay with me."

"I was wondering about the two hats."

"Nick," he said, beating a change of light and

turning a corner effortlessly as the big car purred along underneath us, "my first year as an investigator, the business was so sparse I had to moonlight somehow. I looked around and saw the taxi boys didn't seem to be starvin', so when I applied for the one license I went ahead and applied for the other. Nowadays if I got a gig over in Decatur or down in East Point I just grab a fare on the way. It pays for the gas."

He pulled up in front of a scruffy-looking, but neat, one-story wooden building. The neighborhood was mostly black, but as I got out of the cab with Russell the faces around me didn't have that look of immediate hostility you get used to in Washington, or Philly, or Oakland. Russell went inside the little restaurant, with me right behind him. Slowing my pace to get a better look at him, I took note of the heavy shoulders and broad back. There'd been a bit about him in Hawk's orientation message, and I'd read it on the plane. He had a very solid record from his CIA days, and was said to be not only a weapons expert but a second-dan Black Belter in karate. Even Hawk hadn't completely been able to settle the question of whether or not Russell still worked for the CIA. They tended to hire him, now, a lot more often than they usually hired outsiders.

Breakfast was every bit as good as he'd predicted, and every bit as good as I'd remembered

Southern breakfasts being. We sent the biscuit plate back for seconds, thirds and fourths before we were done. The coffee, miracle of miracles, was good funky chicory stuff, the kind you almost never find more than fifty or sixty miles east or west of the lower Mississippi. Mamie, the owner, was from Memphis, and she believed in carrying your own ambience around with you. If that meant coffee New Orleans style I couldn't agree more. I was on fourths of that, too, by the time Russell decided to talk turkey.

"Okay," he said at last, "here's the scoop. Tomorrow night, accordin' to schedule, Mr. Big is supposed to attend the dinner, and the speech is scheduled for 8:30 . . . ."

"Hey," I said in a low voice, glancing at Mamie's shapely backside as she bussed the table next to ours. "Security? I mean, she can . . . ."

"Nick," Russell said with a patient smile, "Mamie moonlights too. In a depressed economy it's nice to live in a town where there's sufficient opportunity for moonlightin'. When she ain't cookin' eggs she works for me. Ain't that right, baby?" He patted that firm bottom appreciatively.

She turned and gave him a glare, and—hunger out of the way—I gave myself a treat by taking a good look at her for the first time. There was plenty to look at, even in the waitress outfit: so much so that, on closer inspection, you didn't believe in the waitress outfit at all. Her grin was friendly, appraising; ultimately, sexy as hell. "You're Nick, right?'' she said in a fascinating contralto. ''Lou says you're supposed to be pretty good.''

''We'll find out how good we all are tomorrow night,'' Russell said. ''Maybe tonight.''

''I ain't free tonight,'' she said. ''Well, I wasn't, anyhow. What you dudes got rollin'?''

''You ain't got any customers,'' he said. ''Sit down.'' I made room for her beside me. That firm thigh brushed mine, and yeah, there was a little electricity in the contact. She turned to throw a quick smile my way, and the smile was full-lipped and full of brown-eyed warmth. The short Afro hairdo suited her to a T, and the small golden hoops in her ears were the perfect touch against that beautiful high-yellow skin.

''Now,'' Russell said, taking charge for now, ''I got a line on a meeting tonight I want us to stake out. It's . . . .''

''Meeting?'' Mamie looked inquisitive.

''Yeah. It may be the one where they discuss how they're gonna do it. It may be a meeting of the whole group here in town, the one Nick's lookin' for.''

''Do go on,'' I said. I took another sip of the coffee.

''Where?'' Mamie asked.

''Underground Atlanta,'' Russell said. ''Second level down. There's an import shop—Irish linens and that sort of thing. The place closes at nine. The meetin's at ten. You know about Underground Atlanta?''

I nodded. It was a perfectly preserved section of old Atlanta—circa 1885—that'd turned up during some excavation near Five Points. The developers had had the wit to restore it instead of tearing it down. Something else I liked about the South besides breakfast.

Mamie looked at me with another one of those appraising glances, sizing me up. "I guess we're ready to get to business now," she said, and stood up to take off her apron. "I wasn't feelin' much like facin' that lunch crowd nohow." She unhooked from the wall a two-faced sign and hung it on the door; the "Open" side faced inward. "Okay," she said with a wry smile at Russell. "Ready when you are, C.B."

I just sat there. "Lou," I said. "Are you sure you want her in this? I mean, I'm sure if you use her she's tough and competent, but . . . ."

"But what?" they both said, in different tones of voice but otherwise perfectly in phase.

"Did you see the dossier on the guy they call 'Rory O'More'? I mean . . . I don't know how much you've been told . . . ."

"You mean the one about the guy he and his friends lynched in Dublin? Yeah, we both know about that. Look, Nick," Russell said. "Mamie Allen here comes from Alabama and I grew up in Plaquemines Parish down in Luzianne. Her husband Roy was real thick with me in the Army, in Korea. When I got out o' service I heard he'd moved to New Orleans and was workin' with a civil rights movement. He . . . ."

"Oh," I said. "*That* Roy Allen."

I looked at Mamie. Her lips were tightly stretched over her teeth. Her eyes looked a little uptight. Otherwise no reaction.

"Yeah. Well, if you've heard of him you'll appreciate it when I tell you Mamie went through the whole thing with Roy—right up to the day he forgot to pick her up on time and saved her life. Because he let the time slip by, when the crackers shot his car all full of holes up near the state line they only got Roy."

"Only," I said. I covered her tan hand with my white one and gave it a quick squeeze. She shot me a tight smile. "I like that *only*." Roy Allen had been a big loss to the rights movement.

"Yeah. Anyhow, Nick . . . I got a thing 'bout lynch mobs. So does Mamie. And neither one of us scares easy. Not yet anyhow. And both of us want a piece of this particular Mick so bad we can taste it."

"Okay," I said. I got up and went out the door after them. Lou went to start the car while Mamie locked up. I opened the door for her and seated her between us on the wide seat of the Mercury. "How'd you tumble to this gang here, anyhow?" I asked Lou. Mamie's long leg rubbed against mine the whole time. She was one hell of a woman.

"I got a call from Hawk," he said. "Yesterday. And the more he went on, the more familiar the guy sounded. I went down to the FBI office here and read the printouts Hawk had had forwarded." If Russell has access to FBI material on that kind of basis, he's got status. If he's got status he's one of our boys—or somebody with rank in the CIA. "And I asked at the agency. Bagby, the man in charge, says this outfit I'd been tailing as a gun and drug smuggling gang, working for the D.A.'s office, has terrorist connections. And . . . ."

"Therefore," I said, "the FBI and the local police are going to be in on the whole thing tomorrow night, right?"

"Man," Mamie said with a grin, "it's gonna be wall-to-wall cops. They're gonna have to seat the Knights of Columbus in another room. There won't be no room for nobody but cops . . . ." The bum grammar didn't fool me; she was "talkin' trash." One of the things it meant was that she was feeling secure and at home around me.

"Okay," I said, thinking. "And if we're covered there . . . ."

"Then who the hell needs us?" Lou said. He took off, letting us feel the raw power in the big car as it surged forward. "Good question, Nick. If I got anything to say about it, there ain't gonna *be* no tomorrow night as far as these dudes are concerned. You think I spent three months maneuverin' these mothers into position for a bust, and then I'm gonna hand 'em over to the Atlanta Police Department? Or Clarence Kelley? No way . . . ."

I grinned at him. "Lou, you're a man after my own heart. What's on the agenda now?"

"I gotta arrange for some iron," he said. "I got small arms right now. But I want some grenades—smoke and fragmentation—and an M-16. The only way three of us are gonna handle that crowd is to put out firepower like twenty people. And I can't promote the grenades through normal channels or somebody's gonna get the picture we intend to cross 'em up and do the bust a day early. You heeled?" he said.

"To my satisfaction," I said. "But you suit yourself. You obviously know what you're doing. Meanwhile, why don't you drop us off near my hotel? I bought this damn coat for a cover identity named Mr. Bender, who dresses crummy. Now that we're not going to be around for the convention, I don't have to be vetted through under the cover. Mr. Bender can go back into the suitcase. I want something that fits, if there's going to be immediate action. Something that will accommodate Wilhelmina."

"Accommodate *who*?" he asked. I made a quick move: the Luger was in my hand. I grinned and stashed it in its sheath again. "Oh, yeah," Lou Russell said. "Okay. Mamie?"

"I'll help Nick shop for a suit," she said. "These things need the woman's touch."

After I'd been outfitted we went up to my room to make a phone call. I tried David Hawk's number. No answer. I wasn't particularly surprised as I sat on the bed, my back to Mamie, and dialed again. The auxiliary number drew a blank too. Hawk would be over on the Hill, most likely. And probably trying to talk his superiors out of keeping him under wraps all day. I went through a cigarette, trying all the numbers I had just on the odd chance that my hunch was wrong; but by the time I stubbed out the monogrammed smoke and hung up for the last time I knew I wouldn't find him by the phone until evening at best. "Well," I said. "That takes care of duty. Now for some fun."

"Anything special you got in mind?" she said behind me. The tone of voice was definitely not the same.

I turned around.

Mamie Allen stood naked in the middle of the floor, a pile of clothing around her feet. She hadn't had much to take off: a dress, a bra, tiny pink pants.

She was, as I said earlier, a hell of a woman.

The brown eyes watched me with something that was not amusement at all. Their gaze was clear and direct. The stance neither dared me nor invited me. It simply said here I am, Nick. Now it's up to you.

She was long and lean and a luscious golden color all over. Her breasts were high and haughty, and the thoroughly aroused nipples were black and pointed. The belly was flat and rose at the crotch to a tawny bush of curling hair. The legs were lean and the thighs strong. The body was that of an

Olympic athlete—one who also happened to be all woman, and a damned beautiful one too. As she threw her head back, facing me proudly, the gold hoops in her ears dangled and gleamed against the honey-colored skin. "Nick," she said. "I—I wasn't made to do without a man for this long. . . ."

No you weren't, I was thinking as I rose to meet her. You sure as hell weren't.

NINE

TIME PASSED PLEASANTLY enough after that. And after *that?* Well, I wasn't crazy about the idea of getting back to work, just then, but I didn't have much choice in the matter. I had a job to do. So did Mamie.

We grabbed a cab to her place to let her get into working gear. Which turned out to be a formfitting black leotard and tights, with a breakaway dress for the street. Stashed under the breakaway dress in odd places were a variety of weapons which reminded me of my own useful little arsenal. There were differences, of course, but they were the kind of differences professionals have from each other. I liked Hugo; she preferred a razor-sharp switchblade. Where my taste went to good old 9mm Wilhelmina, a gun which could knock you down if it pinked you on one wrist, she preferred something a lady could stow in a stocking if she were in mufti. I noticed, though, that it wasn't any damned ladylike little .25, and I approved. If there's a reliable .25 in the world they have yet to prove it to me.

She caught me looking. So . . . what the hell . . . I gave the rest of her a look too. She gave me an insolent grin for my pains.

"Hey," I said. "You wouldn't be caught dead shucking me, would you?"

"Me? Me shuck anybody?"

"The Chamber of Commerce says Southern folks are straightforward and trustworthy. They have all the Girl Scoutly virtues and no vices at all, and the last thing in the world that would ever occur to one of 'em would be to jive anybody, now."

"Want to see my Girl Scout salute?"

"Okay. What the hell agency are you with?"

"Agency? Man, I work for Lou Russell. I ain't ask'd him who he works for."

"And you're gonna risk your neck on that?"

"Hell, yes. Ain't you?"

I considered the justice of that one. I shrugged.

"Point for your side. I've got a feeling he's okay. And he comes recommended."

"I should hope the hell so. I ain't above guessin'. I've worked for him three times so far. Three times when it counted, anyway." With business on the agenda she was slipping out of the "trash" and into schoolbook English one sentence at a time. "I think he's got some sort of special category. We worked for the Secret Service one time. There was a bomb scare when the president came through. That one didn't make the papers."

"I heard about it. Go on."

"Another time . . . well, you remember the case of the missing nuclear weapon? The plane that jettisoned an H-bomb by mistake off the beach at Savannah?"

"Down at Tybee?"

"That was what they said. They mounted this big damn skin-diver bit, with boats all over the place and the press invited, up off Tybee Light. That was for show. The real operation was down off Ossabaw, where the bomb got dropped. Me and Lou were flown down. We're both cleared for almost anything they do in the Cousteau specials. We got the damn thing loaded on the helicopter with tackle and it was airlifted on one of these big Piasecki jobs over to a tramp oiler with a phony oil tank. They ran the thing around the Keys and unloaded it in secrecy in Corpus Christi. You ever seen an H-bomb, Nick? Fifteen feet long."

"And who did the disarming?" I asked.

"Oh, now, don't look at *me*. Lou Russell's the one who's handy with the pliers and the screwdriver. I can't change a tube on my hi-fi."

"Yeah, yeah. You ready?"

"Let me stash this switchblade between the glossy brown globes of my firm but bountiful bazoom."

"Nasty looking little thing," I said. "The knife, I mean."

"You wait 'til you have a look at what Russell thinks is the latest thing in blades," she said. "A Bowie up one sleeve and a straight razor up the other."

I shuddered inside. God knows I've faced worse weapons. But those damn things have my number. I'll go up against one if I have to, though I won't like it. The last time somebody waved one of those things at me in a fight . . . well, I did what I had to, but I couldn't bear to look at even a Gillette Trac II that close to my Adam's apple for some time afterward.

Outside we grabbed a cab. "You hungry?" she looked at me hopefully. "I know Russell don't eat before trouble, and all. But Nick, baby, I always get hungry after . . . ." One of those brown hands gave my knee a squeeze.

"Mamie," I said, "I'd eat a steer whole right now, if I had to kill him with my bare hands to eat him."

"Don't know about no steers," she said. "How 'bout an all-you-can-eat place that serves boiled shrimp?"

"Boiled in brine? With maybe blackeyed peas 'n' bacon? And rice? And biscuits and honey?"

"Oh, you peeked. You've been down here before."

"Yeah," I said, giving her an appreciative look up and down in that breakaway outfit of hers. "But it's been too damn long between visits. I won't make that mistake again."

By eight-thirty we'd been waiting at the checkpoint we'd set up to meet Russell for maybe twenty minutes. Mamie kept checking her watch, there at the rear of the bus station. "Damn it, Nick," she said. "Lou's never late for anything. Particularly for something like this. I don't like it."

"Everything's *fubar* in this case. Let's cab over to his place. Come on." I grabbed her hand. A couple of rednecks gave us a look, but didn't complain. Atlanta's changed lately.

"Everything's *what*?" she said as I dragged her out the door.

"Old GI terminology from World War II. Initials stand for 'fucked up beyond all recognition.' " I hauled a cab over to the corner with a wave, shoved her inside beside me, and slammed the door. "Give him Lou's address," I said. As she did, I reached inside my coat and loosened Wilhelmina in her holster.

She caught the action. "Hey," she said. "You don't suppose . . . ?"

"I don't suppose anything, honey, until I see

reason for supposing. But I think I'm going to be a long time getting to bed tonight. You're heeled, I know. Keep it loose and accessible. I think there's trouble ahead."

There was. Somehow I had a feeling it would be a familiar kind of trouble, and that turned out to be the case. Lou Russell's office was on the second floor of a funky old office building in a rundown part of town. It was one of those old-fashioned places with white milky glass windows, a lot like David Hawk's office. It looked like any other place on the floor except for the neat sign that said:

LOUIS RUSSELL
Confidential Investigations

RUSSELL ENTERPRISES INC.
Golden Boy Cab Company
Mamie's Restaurant

But that wasn't what really drew your eye just then. The kicker was the splash of red—solid red—that covered three-quarters of the white glass of the window.

"Oh, God," Mamie said.

"You stay here," I said. "Cover the door for me, just in case. I'm going in." I knew damn good and well my birds had flown. But it was one way of keeping her from having to look at something that might well be as bad to look at as, as what had happened to her husband years before.

When I forced the door—they'd locked it from the inside and gone out the window—I saw him immediately. And, damn it, Mamie saw him over my shoulder, too, and let out a sob.

The floor was slick with blood. All over. Lou Russell's blood. They'd let loose so much of it that he must have given up the bulk of it before that tough heart of his stopped pumping. He'd got one of them, too—wild horse that he was—a body lay in the corner, its pockets stripped and turned inside out. There was a hole from a large-caliber gun in the middle of its chest.

But Russell . . . . They'd crucified him from a Victorian hat-rack—one of those damn things with moose horns at the top. His hands had been cut through with a knife at the palms and the prongs of the moose horns had been shoved through the bloody holes. His throat had been cut, along with his wrists. He'd been disemboweled. And castrated.

There was a single knife left there on the scene. It pierced Russell's chest just below the corner of the rib cage. Between the haft and Russell's bloody breast a note was pinned:

> On the green hills of Ulster
> the white cross waves high,
> And the beacon of war throws its
> flames to the sky;
> Now the taunt and the threat let
> the coward endure,
> Our hope is in God and in Rory O'More!
>
> UNION OR DEATH
> *The Red Swineherd*

I looked at Russell again. And I was seeing red. Red for the blood on the walls and the floor. Red for all the blood spilled by these sanguinary bastards. Red for . . . .

Then as I turned my head I saw Mamie at the door. "Goddamn it," I shouted, "I said stay outside, woman."

Her voice was surprisingly calm. And it was about a fifth below her usual tone. "Nick, I've seen this kind of thing before. I—I'm not used to it, but . . . ."

"All right," I said. "But I'll do a snoop around the room. I've got to. There may be something I can learn from it. Meanwhile, you keep me covered out there."

"Okay," she said. Her voice was strong and controlled. "But hurry."

I had a look at the other body. Russell's shot had been dead center. Other than that, and the physical characteristics the FBI would have on the wire back to Hawk by morning, there wasn't much to be seen. I stood up and looked out across the room where the light from the open window gleamed on the trail of bloody footprints that ended at the sill. Two sets of prints . . . .

Clear prints. There was just a chance . . . . I put some newspaper on the floor, enough to keep my knees from getting soaked, and gave the footprints a close look. "Yeah," I said. "Oh, *yeahhhh*" And caught myself up for a second. I'd picked that up from Russell, and I'd only known the guy one day.

Well, he'd been a strong personality. I'd remember him a while. And I'd nail whoever had done this to him.

I scuttled over to the other body. And, hauling out my little pal Hugo, I pried off the brand-new, highly-patterned-on-the-bottom heels on his well-cut, expensive—Regent Street, London—boots and stuck them in my pocket.

But not before I'd noticed, quite clearly, that they were the same as the fragment I'd found in the corridor of the Italian Embassy a couple of days before. Only these were in almost mint condition. There wasn't even any blood on them. Their owner had been plugged by Lou Russell before the bloodletting had begun, and he'd turned up his heels—literally—before there'd been any chance to spoil them.

"Nick," Mamie said. "I—I heard a siren."

"Okay," I said. "Let's get the hell out of here. Come on. We'll go out the window same as they did. I'll put more paper down. They'll wind up questioning you and we don't want your damn footprints in this gore, compounding all the hassle." I got her to the window and we went out and down the fire escape. And, with her expert help, we disappeared, white man and black woman, into the night streets of Atlanta before anyone could trace us to that gory room in that shabby building, and the two dead men inside it.

Twelve blocks away, safe among neon and flashing lights on a major artery leading into the downtown area, I stopped her. "Okay," I said, "this is as far as you're going. The target area's only a block or two away, and I know my way from here."

"Hold on," she said. She turned to me, brown eyes flashing. "If you think I'm gonna hang out on this one, after this evening, you got—"

"You hold on," I cut her off. "This is business, remember? I don't play chivalry games in business matters. If you could be anywhere near as valuable going in there with me to bust things up as you could be doing what I want you to do right now, I'd say go ahead. But Mamie: Did you see me prying those bootheels off the guy's shoes back there?"

"Yeah, but . . . ."

"Well, those boot heels are more important to this investigation than I am. Or you either. They're the only clue we have to where these guys have their HQ. If both of us go in, and both of us get scragged, the whole investigation goes right down the drain. No. Somebody's got to get this stuff to Washington, and in a hurry. Mamie, baby, you're it."

"But . . . ."

"Don't give me any buts. I'm a professional. Lou was a professional. You? You're a wild card. You don't have a damn thing to protect you when the cops move in wanting to know what you know about all this. You also don't have any protection for when the same people who got Lou decide to add you to their list. You've gotta get out of town. I don't want you wandering around with one of those goddamn poems pinned to . . ." I gave her a quick grin. ". . . those aristocratic knockers there."

She tried to smile, but she was still mad. "Look. . . ."

"No, you look. Here, take this." I handed her a blank credit card. "This is an emergency card that will buy you a trip to anywhere people can go, including the moon. Use it. Don't stop off at your pad or anywhere else. You may have visitors you don't want to meet. Get in a cab and head for the airport. They won't be expecting you to blow town. This card will bump any passenger who has the seat you want unless he's Jimmy Carter, and it'll get you to Washington. When you get there call this number." I gave her the code for Hot Line Five. "You say 'sixty-forty' and the other guy will say 'hike.' That code is secure; but call from an isolated phone booth, not through some hotel switchboard just in case."

"What do I say then?"

"Tell him you've got Exhibits A and B and Mr. Russell is doing fine on that farm he bought, and Mr. Carter is alive and well six feet underground in Arlington Cemetery." I reached out and kissed her on the nose. It was a nice nose: strong and Hamitic. "Now go! And take these." I handed over the heels. "Stuff them in your stocking and don't let anything happen to them. If anybody gives you any trouble from here to D.C., shoot him. Cop, or crook, or whoever. The guy in D.C. will pick up all the bills. And he'll have you under guard the minute you call him. Okay?"

"I—I guess so. But Nick . . . ."

"'Bye," I said. "I'm banking on you." I patted that firm bottom and shooed her toward a cab. Then I took off at a rapid clip, not looking back. It was almost time for the big showdown, the one Lou Russell had planned. Only this time there was only going to be one guy ganging up on them. *Me*.

I let a grin slip across my face as I approached the Underground Atlanta kiosk under the street-lights. I liked the odds.

TEN

I HAD ONE moment of apprehension.

There's a brief point when entering Underground Atlanta where you're . . . well, the technical term they call it by in the War College is "enfiladed." If there were a half dozen of you coming down those narrow stairs from the street, all somebody like our playful little Irish pals would have to do is step out of the shadows with an M-16 and gun you down. There wouldn't be a damn thing to hide behind.

Now, coming down the stairs, I had the one quick flash of apprehension. Not exactly a hunch, but I expected somebody down there to step out and rake the stairs with a machine gun. They'd taken Russell, and he was as tough as five guys. And they'd got Considine and he was tougher than Russell. Not smarter perhaps, but tougher.

I got down the stairs, though, and slipped into the shadows by the stairwell to have a look around.

It was pretty much the way I'd expected it to be. Matter of fact, it was an interesting little piece of real estate. I'd like to go back sometime when I'm not working and enjoy it.

But just then it had a feeling of tension for me, and the shadows and highlights of the little crossroads, with its cobbled street and brick walls and unaltered period buildings—way down under the streets of modern Atlanta, like the Roman Forum—which might have seemed picturesque at any other time, looked downright ominous.

The place was closing down for the night.

As I watched, a guy in Gay Nineties getup—striped vest and handlebar mustache—stepped out of his ice cream shop and flipped the "Open" sign around until it read "Closed." He went back inside and rolled a shade down over the window. After a moment or so the light went out. I wondered what this place did for back doors, thirty-five feet down or so; but this guy didn't seem to be coming out again. Either he knew something I didn't or he had a pad of his own in the rear.

At the end of the street, there was some sort of night spot, and it was still going strong. You could hear loud Dixieland music: a trumpet, a trombone, a tuba on the bottom, a clarinet wailing way up in the stratosphere where a clarinet isn't really supposed to play but has to because the brasses are too loud. The next three windows were dark. Then there was a hot dog stand and that was closing too.

Finally I spotted it. One of the doors opened on a sort of arcade, with the signs of several shops posted. The Maddox shop had closed down, but I spotted the Irish linens. I loosened Wilhelmina in her holster and strolled down the street, moving apprehensively from shadow to warm patch of light and back into shadow again under the revamped vintage gaslights. Next door to the arcade a museum of antique coin-operated machines—pianolas, mechanical bands, that sort of thing—stood open, its bright lights cheery in the gloom of the subterranean city. As I passed it I heard somebody's nickel drop and a barrel-organ begin wheezing out a phthisic version of "Springtime in the Rockies." I wondered who'd be playing the machines at this time of night.

The arcade's street-level stores were all dark, but you could see the light was still on down the curving stairwell. Once again, I noticed with some dismay, I'd have to slip down the only visible way there in a totally unprotected situation. I looked around; there didn't seem to be anyone watching. I pulled Wilhelmina and tiptoed down half a flight before stopping to peek cautiously down the stairs.

All clear so far, I thought. I went another half a flight and it was still all clear.

Now there was only the one door before me. It was solid, unlike the glassed doors on the street. The sign said, "Hibernia House. Irish Imports. Fine Linens and China."

There was a light under the door.

I bent over and put one ear to the keyhole; I didn't hear anything then I looked inside, but I couldn't see anything.

I tried the handle . . . it gave.

I should have stopped there, but somehow the hunch thing wasn't working. It's probably some reflex in my system that picks up on sticky vibes then warns me when danger's near. Well, sometimes it works and sometimes it doesn't. It wasn't working that night.

I cracked the door.

A quick peek around showed me only a store that somebody had forgotten to close up completely. All the lights were burning. All the stock was neatly arranged in the bins. Nobody was there.

I stepped inside, Wilhelmina at the ready.

The place was empty.

At the end of the room a second door stood closed. I tiptoed down the corridor past the cash register and stood before it.

I could hear voices inside.

I put my ear close to the door. I could catch an odd phrase here and there.

First voice: ". . . Seal off the side exits just before we move? They could. . . ."

Second voice: "I'll take care o' that." Irish accent. "We'll exit by the door stage left. And look. There's a light complex. If you can blow that. . . ."

Third voice: "Capital. Leave 'em in the dark. They'll panic. Oh, that's capital."

First voice: "Meanwhile we've got the German bastard. Hit him from both sides. If one man misses him from below, the other will get him from above."

Third voice: "And the car picks us all up . . . here."

Second voice: Yes, and I . . . ."

There was a sound from the other end of the store.

I looked up.

There was a man standing there with an M-16 slung over his shoulder. I pulled Wilhelmina.

He didn't have time to draw. He did have time, though, to yank the pin on the hand grenade he held in his hand and heave it my way.

Three seconds to let the handle explode away

and set off the detonator. Three seconds after *that* before it blows your face off, sending high-speed fragments of metal in all directions.

One.

Wilhelmina went horizontal. She pulled even with his chest, his head.

Two.

His hand was clawing at the M-16's sling. I shot him once in the middle of the forehead. A squirt of red shot three feet in front of him and the back of his head painted the wall with a solid splotch. His eyes were still open.

Three.

He started to pitch forward on his face, the light already gone from his eyes. The cotter pin gone, the handle of the grenade made a light clink as it landed against a glass showcase. The grenade landed, bounced once, twice . . . .

Four.

. . . And came to rest in front of my feet. I was already stooping for it.

Five.

I got my hands on it and wheeled, and threw open the door as quickly as I could, heaving the goddamned bomb willy-nilly through the opening and diving on my face.

Six.

I braced for the explosion.

Nothing happened. A dud!

It was good I was on the floor.

There was a hell of a roar inside . . . It was from an M-16, with those super high speed projectiles that make such a mess of you when they hit and an even worse mess when they come out. It traced a thin line across the door right where my belt line would have been if I'd been standing there. Behind me it made a mess of the linen display. It would have cut me in half. As it was I didn't wait around to see what it had done to the door. I was on my belly, scuttling to safety behind a big display case. And as the first of them came around the door I squeezed off a shot at him. It missed, but it was close enough to make him duck back inside.

Keeping low, I sprinted for the stairs.

Behind me, the M-16 spoke again. It cut a furrow down the floor to stop an inch behind me as I dived for safety again. I hit and rolled and came out the other side, and when I came out of the roll there were three of them at the other end of the room and they all had their guns drawn. One held the M-16; the others carried pistols.

I fired point-blank and drilled one of them right through the eye. The 9mm slug hits hard. It bounced him, twisting, off the wall. Once more I had to dive for cover again as the M-16 opened up again . . . and quit.

He'd have to reload. That might buy me precious time.

I slipped one hand inside my belt and reached for Pierre, a gas bomb guaranteed to bring sweet dreams to anybody he meets in a closed room and a moment's stupor, at worst, to a man standing in a working wind tunnel. The present situation was neither. I needed time, though. I heaved Pierre against the wall behind them; he hit and dropped like a stone.

There was a raw curse from down there as the gas went to work. At worst it'd stifle them and make it damned hard for them to breathe . . . hopefully, just long enough for me to make it up those narrow stairs to some sort of safety. I got on hands and knees and dived for the open door.

As I did one of them fired blindly, cursing and coughing. It wasn't my luckiest day.

The bullet hit the floor at a sharp angle and ricocheted, knocking the prop out from under a stack of boxes. They teetered and fell.

One of them landed on my right thigh. My whole leg went numb with a painful charley horse. I couldn't seem to work the thing at all.

I lurched into the stairwell and grabbed the rail, gritting my teeth. I one-legged it one step at a time up to the landing.

Not a moment too soon, either. The M-16 was working again, and I'd barely made it around the corner of the stairs when five rapid-fire shots plowed into the wall behind me. I doubled up on the speed, still unable to get any response but pain out of my right leg. I hoped I could make it to the street before they reached that second landing themselves.

At the street level I leaned on a wall and tried to get that leg to work. I thought I had it operating, and put a little weight on it again . . . but it betrayed me and almost dumped me on my face.

I looked up and down the little underground street. Down the way a whole section of the gas-lights winked off. Couldn't anybody hear all the racket down there? Or did the noise kind of get swallowed up, the way it does inside a mine? Panting, I hopped awkwardly into the street outside and shot a quick glance both ways, looking for shelter.

Almost all of the lights in the street were off. The hot dog stand was dark. The joint with the Dixie band was too far to get to on one leg.

Behind me I could hear curses, and footsteps on the stairs.

I wheeled and fired Wilhelmina at the stairwell. It wasn't intended to hit anyone, just to slow them down. The bullet, took a crazy bounce, however, and winged somebody—how badly I had no way of knowing. It had its effect: It stopped that mad rush out into the street.

I looked around again. There was one other business open in the underground street.

It was that dopey museum for antique musical instruments. Pianos, with player attachments. Barrel organs. Crazy mechanical bands played by metal monkeys.

It was quiet there now. But the lights were still shining brighly.

It was a lousy place to hide.

On the other hand, it was next door. And that leg of mine still played funnybone games on me. I couldn't get it to do anything reliably at all.

I turned and fired another round at the stairs. This time no one was hit. I watched it bounce off and ruin somebody's window.

Then I hopped stupidly out into the street and headed for the pianola joint. As I ducked inside the door I could hear their angry voices out in the street:

First man: "Here, the bastard went that way. . . ."

Third man: "No, no, he can hardly walk. The box fell on his leg. No, he can't have gone that far. Look . . . just look there . . . ."

I didn't like that. It sounded like somebody had things all figured out. I ducked back past a huge barrel organ—Jesus Christ, there must have been three dozen such machines in the joint, and the signs on the walls indicated they were all in some kind of working order. There was a door in the back. Perhaps it led somewhere . . . but when I tried it it was closed tight as a drum.

There was a creaky footstep up front. "Carter?" said the first voice. "It is you, isn't it? We thought we'd got you in Washington. Well, better late than never. There's no way out, Carter. We're coming in. And don't think anyone's going to hear us, and come to the rescue. Stephen? How are ye fixed for nickels?"

"Hmmm . . . here. Damn. That arm's going to be sore for a week."

"You'll survive," the first voice said. "Carter? Still there? Look, I'm going to start all of the machines. By the time we've a dozen or so of them going here nobody'll be able to hear anything at all. Watch." I could hear him fooling with one of the machines. A ragtime piano with a lurchy beat went off into *Weeping Willow*, by Scott Joplin. Another nickel: one of the monkey bands struck up *The Man Who Broke the Bank at Monte Carlo*.

"Carter," he said. "You could save us the bother. You . . . ." But then the other guy started another of the machines: it was the *Springtime in the Rockies* one again. And he was dead right, it was getting loud with all those machines playing all those songs in different keys. I could hear him talking to me as another barrel organ struck up a crazy South American tango, but I could no longer make out the words. And right after that another of the monkey bands went to work on *Under the Double Eagle*.

I crouched on the floor, bum leg extended before me, holding Wilhelmina. I checked my pocket. The extra clip was gone! It must have slipped out during that crazy hegira up the stairs.

How many shots gone? Three? Four?

I moved behind a row of peep-show machines. As I did another pianola struck up *Peg O' My Heart* while a barrel organ, way out of tune, hit *Come Josephine in My Flying Machine*. The sound was as loud as a rock and roll band by now, and sounded almost as bad. I was a sitting duck for the M-16, and there didn't seem to be a damned thing I could do about it.

ELEVEN

I GOT DOWN on the floor, nice and low. With my face almost to the floor I could see under the machines. I watched for their feet. I was thinking of plugging the first one I saw in the foot. That's not the worst wound in the world to have, perhaps—but it's not too far away from it either. Nobody ever succeeds in putting those delicate little bones back together the right way. And you walk around in one kind of pain or another for the rest of your life.

Not that that mattered all that much. I didn't care how these little sweethearts made out the rest of their lives. What I really needed now was to buy some time until my leg got back in operational shape, and if I could cripple one or both of them in the meantime, that was gravy. I kept an eye out, now, Wilhelmina at the ready.

And by God, there was the first set of feet. I thought I was sure it was the guy with the automatic rifle. I lay my cheek flat against the floor and put Wilhelmina in front of my face, trying to draw an accurate bead. I squeezed the trigger, slowly, taking up the slack . . . and damned if there wasn't a pair of woman's shoes just behind, sneaking up on him.

I let up on the trigger. I couldn't take a chance on hitting a stranger. Who was it? Mamie, disobeying me? Well, it could be, in those black stockings and flat canvas shoes; but I thought I remembered Mamie's legs being thinner than that.

There was a loud sound. The guy with the gun let out a yell. The gun went off at the ceiling, tracing a row of holes across it. The music was so loud by now that you could barely make this out. I could see the two pairs of feet scuffling there. I got to my knees and slipped around the machine I was hiding behind.

There was Sinead Geoghegan, expertly putting a judo hold on the guy with the gun. He dropped it to the ground, in pain, and swung his hand around in a vicious karate chop, aimed at her neck.

It never got there. Wilhelmina chalked that one up all by herself. She just up and directed herself in my hand right at the guy's forehead and let go. The 9mm slug of the Luger caught him on one cheek and tore through into his brain. He dropped like a stone. Sinead shrank against the wall, letting him fall.

"Hey!" I said. "Down! There's another of them in here!"

Too late. He'd crept around behind me while the other guy and Sinead were wrestling for the machine gun. And the pistol in his hand spoke once, nice and close to my ear missing me by a foot. It missed Sinead by less; it was her he was aiming at, and it came an inch from cropping that pretty nose of hers. She shrank back behind a muxic box, but there was still a lot of her showing. I whirled and shook Hugo, my pencil-thin stiletto, out into one hand for close-quarters action.

I wasn't quick enough. The gun barrel raked across my face and dropped me on my kisser, with plenty of English on it. And as I knelt there shaking my head he drew another bead on Sinead. I looked up, seeing double, and saw the two images of him leveling the gun on her only half-hidden form.

He pulled the trigger . . . and shot Sean Mulrae in the shoulder. Sean had dived out from cover and into the path of the shot. Seeing what was happening, he'd elected to take the bullet meant for

Sinead. The bullet spun him around, dumped him against one of those crazy machines—it immediately struck up *When Irish Eyes Are Smiling*, cynical bucket of bolts that it was—and slammed him against the far wall.

I should have been faster. As it was, all this happened before I could get Hugo in our foe's guts and give him a twist. After that everything was okay, more or less. I gutted him like a fish. The light went out in his mean smile, just like that. He fell to the ground.

Sinead looked at me.

"Nice work, honey," I said. "But get Mulrae. He's been hit pretty solidly. I'm going to frisk these bums as quick as I can. Then we've got to get Sean to the medic and search the room downstairs before someone calls the police." I went to work on the third man's pockets as I talked.

"Room downstairs?" she asked. But then she got down to business; besides being an angel of mercy who'd probably saved my neck—only to need saving by Mulrae a moment later—she was a professional, and she got to work on Mulrae as quickly as she could. I caught pieces of the conversation as I turned out my man's pockets systematically:

Sinead: "Ah, Mulrae, you're a gallant man for all that. Ah, poor dear. And the bullet was intended for me."

Sean: "Don't give yourself airs, Bridget. I stumbled."

Sinead: "Ah, well, no matter. You came along at a propitious enough time, whether it was by design or not. Here, let me. . . ."

Sean: "Jesus Christ, woman, can't you tell when something hurts?"

Sinead: "Oh, sorry now. We'll make it better. Here. . . ."

Sean: "Ach, mother of God, you've got a touch like bloody King Kong."

Sinead: "Be that as it may, we've got to get you upright. You're going out of here in one piece, I'm thinking. . . ."

Sean: "Jesus, Mary an' Joseph, she thinks I'm a bag of praties. . . ."

I frisked both guys and found nothing of any interest at all. Phony IDs, a pair of wallets, each with twenty dollars in small bills, and a couple of probably phony credit cards made out in the same names as the IDs. The IDs—recent Georgia drivers' licenses—were damned good. You had to look close to spot the sloppy printing in the fine-print sections.

Then, using Hugo as a jimmy, I removed one each of those distinctive boot heels. They were the exact match of the ones I'd taken from the man Russell had killed in his office.

"Okay," I said. "Let's get the hell out of here." I bent over Mulrae. "Sean," I said. "I'm sorry but you won't like this. I'm gonna have to carry you over one shoulder, and I'll try not to joggle you any more than I have to."

"No fear," Mulrae said, his face tight with pain. "You can't hurt me the way Bridget, here, hurts me. She handles me . . . ouch, Jesus . . . it couldn't hurt worse if she had a stevedore's hook in me. . . ."

"Well, I like that," Sinead said. But she straightened up, all business. "I'll be after gettin' up on the street an' hailin' a taxi, Nick. Take care, now." And she was gone.

"Hmm," I said to Mulrae. "Nice girl. I wouldn't be so hard on her." I straightened him up, getting my legs under me. I got him around the ribs and lifted. He swore loudly. I got my shoulder under him and stood up. "Say," I said when his muttering subsided a bit. "How the hell did you manage to trace me?"

"I—I don't have any idea about the woman," he said in a very clenched-teeth sort of voice. "Myself, I can track a drop o' water downriver and not lose it. You're pretty good, Carter, but not so good that I can't follow you."

"Then you didn't come together?" I reached the steps and took them one at a time, feeling every one of Mulrae's pounds with each step. My leg still hurt like hell but it was obeying orders at last.

"Together? Ach, Christ . . . Carter, I work alone. . . . I . . . damn it. . . ."

"Save your breath," I said. We reached the street. Sinead was there with another of those independent cabs, the door standing open. She came forward to help me.

"Nick," she said as we loaded him in, "where do I meet you? You *are* going back to search the room, of course."

They'd done a damn good job of trailing me. Might as well figure the next time I wouldn't give them the slip so easily. "Meet me at the Greenbrier Hotel in an hour. Room three-oh-two."

"Righto," she said, and settled in beside Sean. I shut the door and gave them a quick nod before spinning on one heel to head back to the Underground Atlanta entrance.

I stuck my head back down into that wrecked Irish import shop, poked through the rubble in the back room, and found it. It was a briefcase—by now somewhat the worse for wear—full of papers, all of them encrypted or encoded. I didn't bother trying to dope them out; that takes time and I didn't have any. I picked it up and left.

Out on the street I could hear the sirens wailing. I grabbed the first cab I could and settled into the back seat. I started to say "Hotel Greenbrier," but a little demon in the back of my head said, "Nick, you'd better call Hawk first." I shrugged and told the driver to let me off a block or two up Peachtree from the hotel. I went into a big posh expense-account bar—they're the only kind that have private phone booths any more—and got on the phone to Hot Line Five.

"Yeah?" the voice on the other end said.

"Sixty-forty," I said.

"Hike," David Hawk said. "Where the hell have you been? What have you been up to?"

"Damn busy doings for a dead man," I said. "Russell's dead, but so is the nucleus of the gang. Three of them, operating out of . . . ."

"Out of that Irish linen shop. Yeah, I know. Which three? Describe them." I did. "Hmm," Hawk said. "Not bad. Sorry about Russell, but you're right. With those three gone the Secret Service can handle the Atlanta problem tomorrow. Get down to the air terminal now and . . . ."

"I'm not finished," I said. "I sent you a present. Perfect copies of that ornamental boot heel. I sent them with a chick who works for Russell. She'll be looking you up in about twelve hours. She'll need protection."

"Mamie Allen?" Hawk said.

"I should have known you'd know about her. Anyhow, Mulrae and Geoghegan tailed me here. Geoghegan helped me nab one of them. Mulrae did too, and he took a bullet in the shoulder. I've got her watching out for Mulrae—they'd be reaching the hospital right about now—and I'm thinking of splitting and double-crossing them again. Meanwhile I've got a briefcase full of encrypted papers. How do I get it to you?"

"There's a pouch service from one of the banks there . . . yeah . . . call this number, Nick." He gave me the dope I needed and I wrote it down. "I think those boot heels are the key to what we're looking for—the headquarters of their operation. I got a report from the worldwide network on those damn things. They're a line put out by a shoe-repair supply company in—"

"In Amsterdam," I cut in. "After all, that is the next stop on my agenda."

"No, Amsterdam trip's been scratched. I've got somebody on that one. No, it's even farther out than that."

"It is? Where?"

"Australia."

"Oh, for God's sake."

"Nick, I want you to take off immediately. There's a man in Sydney that I used to work with back in World War II. He's retired now, but he's still fit and he knows more about our end of the racket than anybody half his age in that end of the world. If he's lost half the steam on his fast ball he'll still be a better man to have on a manhunt than virtually anybody outside of AXE. Here's his number." He read off a quick series of numbers and letters. "I think he'll be able to help you trace that down to the station it comes from."

"Station?" I said. "I don't understand."

"The Aussies tend toward large cattle ranches they call stations. They employ vast sums of men. Often each one of these will have a sort of distinctive variant of the standard cattle-station outfit that they wear. The reason is, the boss—the 'squatter' who owns the lease—buys up supplies at one time for a couple of years or so. On a station everybody does his own cobbling and leatherwork. They buy the stuff wholesale, by the large lot. After doing business with the same firm for a number of years they'll sometimes ask for a special lot to be made up with some sort of personalized thing about it—a logo, or a motto, or something similar."

"Hmm," I said. "That's what that funny animal was."

"Yeah. A Tasmanian devil. Of course it comes out sort of crude on a boot heel, done up in hard rubber. But my pal—his name's Alf Beamish, incidentally—thinks that'll turn out to be a positive ID. Get in touch with him immediately. He'll organize whatever sort of operation needs to be organized in order to get inside their HQ and get the hell back out again with the goods. You might like Beamish. He's an old pro, and he has this pal, an old retired black tracker who used to work with the CID there. Way Alf tells it, Jacky could track a nickel through the mint and not lose it. He could track a seagull across the Pacific, a week later, by the shadow the critter made on the water."

"Sounds okay."

"They are. Keep in touch," he said and hung up.

If there's a finer sight in the world than Sydney

and Botany Bay, seen from the air as you settle into the glide path to land, I'm damned if I know what it is. The part of town every tourist knows is the little neck of land between Darling Harbour and Woollomooloo Bay, enclosing the squared-off recess of Sydney Cove and the horseshoe-shaped one of Farm Bay. Inside this trapezoidal spit, as you watch it from that height, it's all shiny white buildings and brilliant green—the Botanical Gardens, the Domain, Hyde Park, Belmore Park, King George Park, the Observatory grounds—and, surrounding them, more blue than you ever saw in your life. Sydney, must have a coastline as long as Chile's with innumerable little inlets and coves and bays, all in use constantly. The Aussies, who have so little inland water, make a big thing of the blue stuff they're surrounded with, and if there's a spot on the Bay that isn't occupied by a collier or an ocean liner you can bet there's an eighteen-footer occupying it, skimming the waves at a hell of a clip with a crew of Diggers half-stinko on fourteen percent beer.

The romance and glamour of faraway places disappears, of course, the moment you hit the airport. All airports are the same. Can't somebody do something about that? The moment I'd cleared customs with a quick flash of another one of my emergency cards, I headed for the cabstand. Somebody was ready and waiting, and even jockeyed his cab over to meet me, pulling the front door open the way they do there. I shrugged and slipped in beside him.

He didn't wait for me to give him a destination. I looked around in some surprise as he pulled away from the curb, the more so since the surge of raw power in that souped-up engine could be felt from the moment he touched to accelerator.

He turned and gave me a lopsided grin. The face was battered, sixtyish. There was one cauliflower ear visible and the nose had been broken at least twice. The eyes were sharp and observant and had more than a slight twinkle in them. The smile managed to be widemouthed and half open in spite of the fact that there was a thoroughly disreputable-looking handmade cigarette hanging from it. "Howjedo, Nick," the raspy voice said.

"Beamish?"

"Too bloodyfucking right. Ready for a bit of work?"

"Yeah," I said. "I got the usual lousy sleep on the plane and I'm nice and out of sorts."

"Good-oh. That's the way we like 'em. What did David tell you, you grumpy barstid?"

"Nothing. Except that you'd know where to find our friends."

"That I do. Over to opal country. South Aussie. Ever heard o' a metropolis called Coober Pedy? It's on the gleaming blue shores of beautiful Lake Cadibarrawirracanna."

"Jesus Christ. I thought there weren't any lakes in Australia."

"Oh, there are. Now and then. I think this 'un had a whole quarter of an inch of water in it for a day or so, three or four years ago." Beamish's voice had an edge on it that might have come from chugalugging battery acid. "Abo names. Coober Pedy means white man in a hole in the ground. Cadibarrawirracanna . . . ."

"You're just showing off. You can't say it with your uppers out, and I've got fifty bucks to back that up."

"Catch an Aussie takin' a bet. You're on, mate, but let me finish."

"Okay."

"Anyhow, we had 'em traced to a cattle station in Queensland. Those boot heels of yours. But somebody blew the cover of the bloke we had watchin' 'em. Somebody sent us our inside man back with 'is head cut off. Another one of them pretty little pieces of verse pinned to his gizzard with an icepick."

"This is where I came in."

"So I understand. Thing is, Nick, I think you an' David got a bad apple in your barrel somewhere. The tip came from D.C."

I sat up sharply, thinking hard about that. He had to be right. There was no other way to explain certain things that had been happening. Lou Russell, for instance . . . . "Go on," I said.

"Thought that'd get to yer. Well, off they went. One of 'em's a new chum, you know. Bought up a lot of property a while back. One of them chunks of property is sittin' right on top of an opal deposit that's been financin' their whole operation most of this year."

"Oh," I said. "We were wondering where the funds were coming from. These guys are not popular on either side of the Irish border, and the American Irish for the most part have never heard of them."

"Well, now you know. Anyhow. . . ."

"That's where we're going?" I asked, not looking forward to it. The opal country is in as desolate a section of Australia as you could ask to see. The area he'd mentioned was a couple of hundred miles south of the exact geographical center, an area so remote and so useless—until the opal diggings were found, anyhow—that the aborigines still controlled the fringes of one side of it and the other side was mainly used as a missile range.

"Soon's we pick up my friend Jacky."

"Okay," I said, and settled back into the comfortable seat of the Jaguar, feeling the powerful engine hum beneath us. Thinking.

A spy inside our system? But who? Mulrae? Sinead Geoghegan? Who else was there?

And another thing hit me. If the Aussie informant's cover was blown, so was mine. If they knew about the local surveillance from a D.C. source, they'd also know about the elaborate story David had worked up about my heroic death. AXE had paid for a cheap funeral in vain.

I was alive again. What a lousy break.

TWELVE

"HERE," BEAMISH SAID. "You're lookin' crook, Nick. Look like you'd seen a ghost."

"I have," I said. "My own. Never mind. Where can I get to a phone?"

"You're gonna call David? Not to fret. I already passed on the word. Diplomatic pouch, Code 23, left this morning."

I looked at Beamish with a new eye. "Good on you, Alf." I chewed on that one for a moment. "I'm brushing up on my Aussie. Or should I have said "'Bloodyfucking good on you?' "

"That's one for the learned professors of Colloquial Orstrylian, Nick. But look, here we are." He turned the car into a downright imperial-looking driveway. The gates were open and everything looked on the up and up until my practiced eye caught the armed guards stationed unobtrusively behind a bush. We pulled up in front of the sort of house a duke, perhaps, or some other gent with sixteen quarterings and a page of his own in Burke's used to be able to afford.

"Come on," Beamish said. And he was right behind me as I skipped up the wide stairs. When the door opened I already had figured out something was wrong, but it was a little late for doing anything about it. Beamish's gun—a damned big one, you can feel the weight of those things—was already stuck in my kidney, hard, and that rough voice had picked up the mellifluous tones of an actor as he said: "All right, Carter. Inside. There's a good boy."

I looked at the second one. He had a Webley pointed at my guts. It didn't seem the time to play games. "Okay," I said. "I didn't quite believe your Aussie number in the first place. It's not bad all in all, but it's a little stagey. Where'd you get the training? Dublin Abbey Players?"

"Old Vic," he said. "It's nice to know the British are good for something in the world." Under the beautifully modulated tone there was a hard edge. "This way."

The two of them sandwiched me as we went through a sort of Grand Hall with the enormous staircase, and approached a first-floor room made of paneled oak. The guy who'd met me at the door opened this one for me. I hesitated, but all it bought me was the gun in the kidney again.

Across the room a man was sitting behind a big desk. He wore gloves. I'd seen him before. The phony mustache and wig were gone, replaced by what looked like yet another and more subtle kind of makeup. I shot a look at the ears, but couldn't make out anything. The hair—again a wig, I'd bet on it—was frizzy and came down over them at the top, and the thick, and obviously phony, sideburns completed the coverup. I knew him by the eyes as well as the gloves. "Daniel O'Grady," I said. He nodded. The two guys positioned themselves behind me, one at each heel, once they'd set me up in front of O'Grady's desk.

"Carter," O'Grady said. "You've become a problem. What shall we do with you?" The face was a little odd. Some of it was real. The nose wasn't; it was a good putty job. The mouth moved wrong. Maybe it had before; I hadn't noticed.

"You're the magician, Marconi," I said, sarcastically. "You could always make me disappear."

"Clever," he said. "Or saw you in half? Well, we'll leave it to our friends at Coober Pedy. They have a knack for the unusual and the poetic in these matters. We've an aeroplane leaving for there shortly. I'll make them a present of you, I think. They owe you something for the affair in Atlanta. They lost a few friends there."

"I lost a friend there, too," I said. "I couldn't make up for losing Russell if I towed Ireland out to sea and sank it, with every man and boy aboard."

"Be that as it may," O'Grady said, "your own usefulness to AXE is ended, obviously. The reason has little to do with whether we kill you here or over in South Australia. The main thing is, AXE is out of business, and for good."

"You're bluffing," I said.

"I'm afraid not," O'Grady said. "By the same token, Northern Ireland is out of business. British rule in Ireland is out of business. If all this doesn't come true in three days' time, New York—and perhaps the entire Eastern seaboard, or even the United States—all of these are likely to be out of business."

"Big talk," I said. But my voice didn't carry much conviction. He was too confident. "Go on."

O'Grady stood up. There was a strange glint in his eye; he was working his way up to something a little at a time. Apparently this wouldn't work if he couldn't walk around a bit and wave his arms. At the moment they were behind his back. His hands seemed curiously wooden, immobile inside those gloves. "Carter," he said. "Have you ever heard of Codeword Omega? Operation Doomsday?"

"No," I said. "I don't have the Guinness Book memorized either. Go on."

"Well," he said. The voice was a trifle louder. It

had a certain controlled intensity that was a little unsettling. "Around six months ago, the first unmanned round-trip flight to the planet Mars was completed. It . . . ."

"I'd heard of *that*," I said. "But what . . . ."

He paid me no attention at all. "The Mars landing and its aftermath were widely publicized, of course. But the essential facts were left out. Or distorted. Or covered up with outright lies in the name of security. The real nature of the mission, and what the scientists learned from it, were, and remain, cloaked in the utmost secrecy."

"Oh?"

"This took many forms. The central one, however, had to do with the official word, broadcast to the entire world, that no sign of life whatsoever had been found on Mars."

"Huh," I said. "And this wasn't true?"

"In fact," O'Grady said, his voice rising, "what the Mars lander found was traces of an alien form of life existing on what at first appeared to be the simplest level. It apparently is not native to Mars, and its makeup contains elements which, at the time of our launch, were not to be found in the atomic table as we knew it."

I let this pass. I watched O'Grady, hands still behind his back, pace back and forth in front of me.

"Obviously," he said, "It comes from some other world—although the scientists conducting the space probe have no idea which one. They don't even know if it comes from our own solar system. That doesn't matter at this point. What matters is that the life-form—a sort of metafungus, spread by spores from one world to another—has some unusual properties. These became immediately evident as the scientists at the space laboratory tried to study the organism."

"What kind of properties?" I asked. He ignored me again. This wasn't a conversation, it was an oration, and it was building up a fine head of steam.

"It turns out that the organism has a strange affinity with animal tissue," he went on. "Let the slightest fragment of the fungoid tissue touch living flesh—be it animal or human—and a strange reaction takes place. It doesn't exactly consume the Terraform flesh, as food, you know. The effect on the unfortunate creature to whom the flesh belongs, however, remains the same as if it had been, in fact, eaten. The effect on the fungoid tissue is totally different. It absorbs—*becomes* part of the flesh of the creature with which it combines. And apparently it assumes the characteristics of that creature, once the spread—which is amazingly quick, mind you—has been completed. It seems to take over the instincts, and even memory, of the flesh it has combined with. Laboratory animals attacked by the spores changed into horrible variants of the things they had been—but the horrible variants now had the characteristics of the animals themselves. A laboratory rat, infected and replaced by the fungoid organism, knows everything a laboratory rat knows—only now it is also inhabited by a strange and alien intelligence so enigmatic that we have little way of communicating with it at all."

"God almighty," I said.

"So far," O'Grady said, "the scientists have kept this organism confined inside the laboratories, in the strictest secrecy, under the most carefully controlled conditions. Once, just once, a human was infected. The human killed himself. The body was burned under the most carefully supervised conditions. You may imagine how seriously the government—that small part of the government which knows about this—takes the entire operation. One scientist, claiming the secret was too important to keep under wraps, announced he was going to blow the operation to the press. He was eliminated on the spot by security men inside the project. He was not even given the chance to finish his little oration, much less to get outside with the news." His voice was coming much more quickly now; the words were clipped, the stage-Irish accent was gone, replaced by a sort of half-English, half-American accent.

"And?" I said. "What has this to do with . . ."

"Ah," O'Grady said. He turned to face me, those strange eyes on mine. "You begin to perceive the ultimate danger of the spores being released. We have no idea how adaptable they are to the climates of Earth. They could be killed by the first frost, but that seems unlikely: after all, they survived much worse temperatures on the surface of Mars, albeit in a dormant state. Then again, they could be killed by certain bacteria or other microorganisms here. Or . . . ." The glint in his eye positively glowed. "They could mean the end. The end of life on earth as we know it."

"Jesus Christ," was all I could say.

"Ah, now," O'Grady said. The voice was high-pitched and tense. "You begin to understand. You begin to see. As the world will begin to see. . . ." He looked up at the clock on the wall. "Around . . . oh . . . twelve hours from now."

"Twelve hours?" I said. "I don't get it."

"You don't understand? You don't see? You fool! You idiot! *We* have it! *We have the Doomsday Spore!*" It was almost a scream. "And in twelve hours the first message is going out! Either our demands are met in full—British off the Islands, Ulstermen and Orangemen moved out bag and baggage immediately, a United Nations guarantee of our complete and unconditional sovereignty forever—or we'll release it! Right in the middle of New York! We'll let it go, from a place where it'll get maximum dispersion! Where it'll spread to the whole city within days! Inside weeks half the people in the area will be affected! Inside months—all!"

My throat was hoarse. I didn't sound at all confident when I said, "Bullshit!"

"Ah!" O'Grady said. He stopped in front of me. "So I'm lying, am I? Bluffing? Making claims I can't deliver? Well, we'll see, Carter! We'll see!" He strode to the end of the room, where a large television was—one of those things with the magnifier on front. The picture was maybe four feet across. He switched it on. "Look!" he said. "This is a videotape made in New Jersey, at a place we've since vacated, two days ago. You may recognize the person, Carter. Judge for yourself whether we're lying!"

The face came on screen.

I recognized it all right. And there he was—the rat inside AXE. Mack Halloran. N24! One of Hawk's most trusted agents! He stood against a wall. He was drugged to the eyes. His voice came out in a monotone, answering the questions put to him by someone offscreen:

Voice: Who stole the Spore?

Mack: I did. Me and three agents of Red Swineherd.

Voice: How was this done?

Mack: For money I leaked out the information about it. Then the R.S. agents grabbed my wife and child. They said that my family would be killed if I didn't cooperate. I was to get into the files and . . . .

Voice: Who inside the NASA lab compromised the project? Who leaked it all out to you?

Mack: Ellen Forsyth. She and I had been

having an affair. She did it for me. I told her it was for security purposes. By the time she found out I was lying it was too late. The Red Swineherd had the Spore.
Voice: What happened to Ellen Forsyth?
Mack: O'Grady . . . O'Grady fed her to the Spore. It—it was awful. She was . . . all over gray stuff. It had eaten away most of her body. . . .
Voice: Has AXE spotted your absence?
Mack: Red Swineherd agents are replacing me and making reports. David Hawk thinks I'm chasing them down in Amsterdam. My double . . . he looks and sounds exactly like me. He . . . .
Voice: What will happen to you now?
Mack: (He starts to say something; then, his face still wooden, he holds up one hand. It is covered with a spongy gray matter. It looks like a terrycloth glove, with fingers and nails. The hand claws at his collar and pulls it open. Inside we can see more of the gray matter, spreading . . . .)

"Jesus Christ," I said again.

"You see?" O'Grady said. He was almost dancing now. *"You see?"* The face still didn't move right, and the voice wasn't the way I'd remembered it. What, I wondered, did the real O'Grady look like? I'd never seen him without makeup.

And . . . God, he could be almost anybody.

"Well!" he said. "That's about it, Carter. You can't stop us—not you or Hawk or anybody. You're all out of business, you see? We've got you right where we want you. When the message goes out there'll be panics. The streets of New York will be a vast, milling mass of frightened people, trying to get out of town. But it won't do any good. The Spore will get loose—if you don't go along with us—it'll get loose and spread."

"Look," I said. "That deadline. You said three days?"

"Yes!" The voice was shrill now. The words came abnormally fast. I wondered idly for a second just what it was that he was on right now. Some kind of upper? Or was it just the crazies? By now I believed him capable of anything. "At noon precisely three days from now. That's New York time. The world has precisely that long to capitulate! *Three days . . . !*" The voice was feverish, the eyes out of focus.

I shook my head to clear it. Then I got mad.

"O'Grady," I said, "I've never heard such a load of crap in my life. I. . . ."

Maybe if I'd been able to finish it I might have managed to put some conviction in it, conviction that I definitely didn't feel. Because it was real all right, and O'Grady was damn serious, and just as sure as I was standing there I knew that they could and would do everything they said they'd do. But I didn't get a chance to polish off the rest of my thought. First one of the guys behind me clubbed me to my knees, then the other whacked me from the other side.

Coober Pedy not only lies in the middle of a bombing range—the vast Woomera missile-testing range, northwest of Adelaide and due south of Alice Springs, in the dead center of the vast and empty Australian continent—but also squarely in the middle of some of the least promising country in the world. If it hadn't been for the opal strikes at Coober Pedy there'd be little reason for anyone to stick his nose that far inland. To one side is the Great Victoria Desert and the aptly named Nullarbor Plain. To ther other is the dry-lake area, with places like Lake Eyre (a gleaming saltpan without a drop of the drinkable in it anywhere) and the Simpson Desert.

When I woke up, arms strapped to my sides around a rear seat in a six-seater light plane, I could see out of the window all right. Right down on the damn dry country. We were circling to land, and as we banked I could see the anthills dotting the sandy plain: white anthills with people digging inside them, as much as fifty feet down. On the squat hilltops other, richer people took the easy way out and dug with bulldozers, slicing into the rubbled plain and going over the dug-up portion afterwards, looking for traces of the precious stones. There was a sort of town there—with dust all over everything—but that obviously wasn't where we were going. Instead, we landed some miles out, in as empty a place as I've ever hoped to see. There was an airstrip, with what looked like a shed at the end and that was about it. When we'd taxied to a half they let my arms loose, leaving the plastic garbage-can-tie handcuffs on my wrists. I cursed them, getting out; those things yanked my wrists so tight together it felt as if my shoulders were out of joint. I got down somehow, staggered around in the blazing sun, and was shoved into the shed.

Then came the surprise. I'd forgotten about Coober Pedy. Everybody lives underground: in houses, apartments, even storage buildings dug into sandy clay stone. It's the only way to keep cool there; outside, the daytime temperatures average way up above a hundred degrees, but it's passably cool down under the stone. And if you're lucky, digging a hole for your house, you may wind up getting rich on the opal deposits you find in the stuff you throw out. Here below the shed was something like an office building, only the walls were made out of clay and the stairs went down, not up. The two guys who brought me over from Sydney shoved me down the stairs, letting me bounce off the walls on the way. At the bottom they picked me up, nice and rough, and threw me through a door into a room. When I struggled to my knees somebody socked me again, and off I went.

The shots woke me up. I could see light under the door of the dark room; I crawled closer to it, painfully. There was a lot of noise out in the hall. Somebody said, "In there! Look out!" and there was another pair of shots. I could hear feet pounding dully on the floor. Another voice said, "Here, you . . . ." and a door slammed.

Time passed.

Down the hall a door opened. There was a roar of laughter: coarse, mean laughter.

There was a shriek. A woman's shriek. Then the door slammed again.

More time passed.

I'd slipped off a bit—too tired not to sleep by now, despite the pain throughout my body—and I was dreaming bad, bad dreams. There was this gray creature that looked like a compost heap. It lumbered like a bear in slow motion. It was coming after me. If it touched me—just once . . .

The door opened. In the blinding light that flooded the room stood a woman. She was naked and disheveled, and her body was covered with small cuts and bruises. She was bleeding in more than a dozen places. Her hair hung in her eyes.

She stood there like that for only a moment. Then two pairs of hands, behind her, shoved her roughly into the room. She fell heavily on top of me. Then the door slammed again, plunging us into pitch darkness broken only by the tiny sliver of light underneath the door.

I struggled to a sitting position. The woman

rolled off me, backing away toward the far wall. "Stay away," she said. "Just stay over there, damn you . . . ."

"Hey," I said. "Easy, Sinead. It's Nick. And how the hell did you get here?"

THIRTEEN

"NICK!" SHE SAID. The edge was still in her voice, but as she groped for me in the dark and threw her arms around my neck, pressing that nice soft firm body to mine, something seemed to give inside her and she burst into tears. I let her sob for a minute or so; then she got control of herself again. "Nick . . . what's the matter. . . ."

"My hands," I said. "They're cuffed. I can't feel my fingers any more. Do you think you could . . ."

"Yes, yes," she said, scrambling back around behind me. "Here."

Now, with my hands in front of me for a change and with Sinead rubbing my chafed wrists and slapping my hands to get the circulation going, I began to feel a little more like a man and a little less like a sewed-up Thanksgiving turkey ready for the oven. I reached inside my coat—and of course Hugo and Pierre and Wilhelmina were all gone. "Damn," I said.

"Yes," she said. "Damn. I could think of a stronger word, perhaps, if I put my mind to it."

"Here," I said. "Try this coat on for size. What happened to your clothes?"

"They caught me spying. I . . . they raped me. One at a time." Her voice was bitter and hard under the lovely Irish lilt.

"Sons of bitches. Somebody's going to pay for that. But how did you get here?"

"I had a tip. Nick, you lost me this time. But Nick. There was a leak in the system. In AXE."

"Yeah, I know. Mack Halloran. Poor bastard."

"What do you mean?"

"What do you know about Codeword Omega?"

"Nothing. Why?"

I told her. All of it, including the little game O'Grady was playing—and which had already begun. "God almighty," I said. "What time is it? What day is it? How much time do we have left? He said twelve hours . . . ."

"I'm not sure," she said. "Jesus, Mary and

Joseph, Nick. Give or take an hour or two . . . that message of his will be going out in . . . Nick, it'll be going out right about now. And here we are . . . ."

"Yeah," I said. "Damn, damn, damn. What else do we need to know? Oh, yeah. That tip you had. It couldn't be Halloran. Who was it?"

"Well, one of our people has a bug on David Hawk. And he knows about Coober Pedy. It turns out somebody found Alf Beamish's body in Sydney this morning. Found Alf, anyway, and he died about ten minutes after the police found him. I was too late to intercept you at the airport, so I came here. And Jesus in heaven, Nick, look at me. Fine operative I am, getting caught like this."

Hell, I wished I *could* look at her. The glimpse I'd got of her, framed in the doorway, had been something special. "It happens to the best of us," I said. "Look at me, walking into a trap like that."

"Oh, come off it. You spotted the fake Beamish the moment you got in the car."

"Okay, I did. And I knew he was going to take me someplace interesting, where I'd learn something. Hell, I've never heard phonier Aussie slang in my life, and the accent was a little off, too. They're not all as good at the game as O'Grady. You could drop him in my lap and I wouldn't recognize him, not until he looked me in the eye." I snorted at myself. "But letting myself get set up for a sucker punch like that . . . ."

"Spilt milk, Nick. But now we've got to get out of here."

"The question is how. What do you know of this joint? How thick are the walls?

"A foot or two. You could dig through." Her hand went to my middle. "Yes, your belt buckle should do to dig through the clay. But they'll be back before you can get much done."

I scrabbled over to the near wall and felt the clay. "You're right," I said. "That's out."

"Here, take your coat back."

"My coat?" I said, not sure what she was planning.

"Of course, you big ninny. Let's see if I can interest them in my fair body again. The bastard that threw me in here . . . he didn't have a turn at me." Her tone was bitter, but controlled. "Nick, you get behind the door there. I'll put up a bit of a screech, and when he opens the door I'll see if I can give him a nice centerfold pose that'll hold his attention for a moment. But when you pop him one, Nick, give him another one for me."

"You're on." I moved into place—and then almost went out of my skull. I'd forgetten that the female voice could give off a howl like that. It was the sort of thing that'd leave a crystal chandelier in tiny pieces all over the floor.

It had its effect on somebody outside, too. There was a scuffle of moving feet; then the deadbolt lock shot back and the door flew open.

And there she was, spread out on the floor, legs wide apart, hands holding herself open, a look of utterly abandoned runaway lechery on her pretty face. And it stopped him dead, all right. His head poked in the door just enough for me to belt him one right behind the ear. His eyes went glassy and he went down. I didn't wait for him to hit. I dived for the door and grabbed the second one by the legs. It got him off balance and he went down, the gun flying from his hand and bouncing on the rug-covered clay floor. He managed to get his hands around my neck, and he might have done quite a job of strangling me if I hadn't creamed him with a short, bruising right to the cheek. I looked up to Sinead, virtually taking the third guy's head off with a high kick. Her bare heel caught him right on the point of the chin and slammed him against a wall. She moved in and gave him two quick fists right under the juncture of the ribs. The air went out of him and his eyes rolled back in his head; he was out before he hit the ground.

"Hey," I said. "Not bad." I grabbed the gun off the floor and, just for the hell of it, frisked the second guy. I came up with a pair of brass knucks, a .25 automatic, and—wonder of wonders—my little pal Pierre. Then I shook the others down. The first man had Hugo, and the one she'd slugged had had Wilhelmina in his hand when he went down.

She caught me grinning. "What's so funny?" she said. She was stripping the smallest one for his clothes. As I watched—a trifle ruefully—she slipped his sweater over her head.

"My own weapons," I said. "I was going to say I felt naked without them." I had a look at her up and down as she stepped into the guy's pants. The bottom half of her was as nice as the top.

"Oh, go on with you," she said. She zipped up the pants and stepped into the guy's canvas shoes, sockless. They were a bit too big, but they'd do for getting around. "Pass me that .25, Nick." I tossed it to her, not thinking. If I'd thought about it I might have hesitated a little. She caught the little gun deftly, worked the slide two-handed, and, drilled all three of them through the head, efficiently and dispassionately. No, the last word doesn't fit. She looked up at me with her features all calm and controlled. "Two of these were in O'Grady's gang when they killed my husband and children," she said. "The third . . . well, I had another score of my own to settle with him after today."

I whistled. "Right. Now let's get the hell out of here." Not a moment too soon, either. I heard footsteps down the way. When I saw feet pounding down the stairs I shoved her back behind a mess of vertical electrical conduits and stepped in beside her, Wilhelmina at the ready.

There were two of them. The first one went past. He got three steps beyond us before she shot him neatly right under the ear. The other one couldn't stop quite in time and stumbled past my hiding place. He took a 9mm slug right in the kisser. "Come on," I said, and took off for the stairs.

"No, Nick!" her voice had an urgent edge on it. I looked around. "No, there's another way out. If there are any of them around now they'll be coming from that direction. Come this way. This comes up at the other end of the runway."

"Okay," I said. "I'm a stranger here myself." I took out after her, watching that nice body of hers move under the men's clothes. I still had a few ambitions about getting to know her better.

The other staircase was around the bend and down a long hall. She increased the pace, and I had to stretch myself a bit to keep up with her. As I did somebody poked his head out of a side room and I ran squarely into him.

Toughest damn Irishman I ever saw. It was like running into a brick wall. And he recovered even before I did. Recovered—and hauled me back into that side room and, his big hands holding my coat, literally threw me all the way across the room to bang off a wall. I'd stowed all my arms; I'd hardly had time to use any of them anyhow before he plowed into me again, this time catching me one with a fist the size of a picnic ham. I saw stars; I was damn lucky I could still stand up. I covered up and backpedaled; he came after me. As he did I stuck out a straight left and caught him on the snout. It was just enough to make him blink, and bring the bright blood down his upper lip. The blink gave me time to spin away and, on the way out of his reach, clip him one on the point of the jaw. He winced, shaking his head. *Glass jaw* I thought. *Now all I've got to do is keep from getting pulverized while I tried to sock him on that nice weak spot*. As I pondered this he feinted with the left and crossed the right. I felt like I'd been hit by a train. I shook my head and worked at getting some strength back in my knees, which were wobbly as hell. Instinctively I swung, leading with the right, and he walked right into it.

Three things happened, all at the same time.

My fist caught him right in the middle of that broad forehead. It not only had all my weight behind it on one end, but all his weight on the other. He ran right into it.

There was a hell of a noise in the small room.

And the big Mick toppled right into me, the momentum of his mad rush carrying him right into my arms. And then I was holding a dead man. I let him fall.

For a moment there I thought maybe I'd killed him with one punch—that's happened before, freaky piece of luck though it is—and then I saw the three tightly spaced bullet holes in his back.

I looked over at the open door. Sinead was reloading with loose shells from the pocket of the pants she was wearing. "Come on, Nick," she said. "The radio shack's down this way."

Radio shack! "Great," I said. "We'd better call David."

"Righto," she said. "Then it's a matter of getting out of here. Come along." I was right behind her as she jogged down the hall. I was breathing hard: that big moose had packed a punch like Ken Norton. Sinead wasn't even winded.

"Here," she said. We slipped into another room that led off the hall. There was a big, efficient old Hallicrafters there. I cut it on and let it start warming up. "I'll keep a lookout," she told me stepping into the hall.

"Does this thing have an antenna?" I wondered aloud. "I can't imagine the signal carrying far without it. Maybe I can raise Canberra."

"You can raise Washington or London," she said. "Or Dublin or Capetown. Just because you don't see an antenna standing up in the air doesn't mean there isn't one. All that mulga scrub out there . . . . It's an antenna field. Directional antennas. The one headed back to the States is perhaps a mile long."

Well, "Beamish" had said they had money. I got on the wire and had David on the air in a moment. He sounded pretty much the way he always did. I could picture his perfect poker face, not even blinking when I told him about all of it—O'Grady, the Doomsday Spore, everything. He did blink—so loud I could almost hear it—when I told him about Halloran.

"I don't believe it," he said.

"You've got to," I said. "I saw him."

"You saw a movie," Hawk said. "I know Mack is missing. I know he's had problems. I had been thinking of giving him a leave. But he wouldn't do this."

"You think this spore stuff is a fake?"

"No, I don't. There is a sample of the stuff

missing. We didn't know what had happened to it. And, yes, it is every bit as bad as O'Grady says it is. But the question is, does O'Grady have it . . . or is he faking?"

"If he isn't, how the hell do they know about the spore?"

"Damned if I know. Maybe the film was faked up to protect the real source."

"In the meantime that statement of his is going on the air any minute now."

"It's already been on."

"And you let me jabber away?"

"There was a good chance you knew something they weren't saying. Hunch turned out to be right. You did."

"Okay. But we have to find out if it's all real."

"Yeah. But in the meantime we have to act as if it were real as hell."

"And plug up that hole. Sinead's here and she says there's a bug on your office. She must have put it there while we were having coffee."

"Righto," she said from the door.

"It's okay," Hawk said. "I caught it this morning. Tell her good work. If she hadn't bugged us I'd have sent her back to Dublin on the first plane out from Dulles and asked the Irish government for a better operative." She saluted him from the door, one eye still on the hall. "Okay. Get the hell out of there. Both of you. Get back here as quick as you can. We've only got three days."

"Yes, sir," I said and signed off. I took off the

phones I'd used to zero-beat the signal. "You heard the man," I said. "Now all we've got to do is get out of Coober Pedy." But when I looked at her she was staring wide-eyed at the wall. When the big Irishman had bounced me against it, the weight of my body had jarred some of the clay loose. There was a flash of brilliant color peeping through the red clay in the exact center of the hole.

I went over and dug it out and weighed it in my hand before handing it to her. "Here," I said. "A little souvenir of your happy vacation on the gleaming shores of exotic Lake Cadiberrawirracanna," I said.

"Jesus, Mary an' Joseph," she said. "What is it?"

"An opal. Biggest damn thing I ever saw. If it's as perfect as I think it is . . . between eighty and a hundred carats. Maybe $10,000." I looked down at it in her hand. Would it pay her for her trouble? I thought not. Apparently I was right. She tossed it in a corner.

"Here, Nick," she said. "Let's go up to the storeroom. Maybe there are some explosives there. We've got to close this place down."

"Just what I was thinking," I said. But I gave the opal a second glance as she went out the door and, just for the hell of it, stuck it in my pocket as I followed her.

We took an airliner to Los Angeles, having first promoted a ride to Sydney with the Aussie CID. In

L.A. we changed lines and took a dogleg flight to Atlanta. There was an hour layover; while we were there it occurred to me to call the hospital and see if Mulrae was still there. To my surprise they patched us right through.

"How are you?" I asked.

"Bloody awful," he complained. "Medics found some complications. Keep sending me back for tests. I'm going out the bloody window one of these days. And you?"

"Things are popping," I said. "We had a little vacation in Australia."

"Oh, good," he said. "Heard about that. Most of it, anyway. Your friend Hawk found my bug this morning and spoiled our day for us."

"*Your* bug."

"Righto. And just when it was getting interesting. Well, as I say, I'm going over the wall. Don't dare say when or how. Nuns watch me like hawks. And speaking of the bloody Pope, is Her Ladyship with you?"

"Yeah." I'll put her on.

"Hello, Mulrae," she said. The voice wasn't hostile, just businesslike. "You're better?"

"I'll say I am, the Sisters of Bloody Whatever say I'm not. Enough trouble mending without a lot of Brides of Christ getting underfoot. No . . . now don't get your back up, luv. I wanted to say something."

"Yes?"

"Only that if you don't leave O'Grady to me I'll

break every bone in your pretty body and drop you off an airplane a hundred miles off Newfoundland."

"Not a chance, Mulrae. He's mine."

"Woman. Do you know the extent of the debt I owe him?"

"No. He killed my husband and children."

"Ahhh." Mulrae's answer was a sigh. "Then I'd like to leave him to you, but I can't. I've got to have his damnable blood, for the sake of the blood that's in me. If I don't kill O'Grady myself my hands'll never be clean again."

"That's about the way I feel myself," Sinead said. "What's your connection?"

"When O'Grady was twenty he wasn't a damn bit better than he is now. He was on the run and my mother hid him. He disappeared. Then he came back a year later, his hands still dirty from a killin', and wanted to take it all up again. She said no. He killed her and threw me in a garbage can. I was six weeks old. I grew up in an orphanage. I was twenty-two before I knew who I was."

"And who are you?" she said. Her voice was husky.

Mulrae's tone dripped icicles and venom. "O'Grady's bastard," he said. "And I'll never be a whole man until I've killed him with my own two hands."

FOURTEEN

WHEN HE'D HUNG up Sinead just stood there for a moment, the phone still in her hand, her eyes a little out of focus. Her face had never looked lovelier, soft and vulnerable; and the clothes we'd picked up for her in Sydney were demure and sexy at the same time, with a lot of emphasis on the bosom right below a girlish collar with a lace fringe on it. She looked around at me and the look was still in her eyes, hurt and puzzled. I had to remind myself that she was obviously a third degree black belt at karate and had murdered five men right before my eyes, as cool as a cucumber. "Oh, God, Nick," she said. "The poor man. What a thing to be haunted by."

I nodded. "We all have our reasons for getting into the racket, honey," I said. I didn't say anything about mine. That was an old, old business, with cobwebs all over it, and the last thing in the world I wanted to do was talk about it. "After a while it gets to be a matter of good guys and bad guys, just like the westerns. It's not quite as easy. I've been working on trying to get the bad guys to wear black hats, but . . . ."

She began slowly to smile, but there was still that hurt look in her eyes. She had begun to understand that there were degrees and degrees of pain. "Nick. You'll always be after making a joke." It was, as it turned out, an affectionate sort of smile. "But you know," she said, "that's the trouble here. The white hats and the black hats . . . they're all mixed up. No, I don't mean O'Grady. We all know where he stands. But there's Mack Halloran. Where does he stand? Does he wear a white hat or a black one? We don't really know yet. David Hawk says Halloran can't have done it. And then there's the fact that . . . ." The look in her eyes finished the sentence.

Oh, how right she was. It didn't matter a damn whether Mack Halloran was one of the white hats or one of the black. Whatever he was, they had him, and he was either dead by now or marked for death. No, Mack wasn't the problem.

The problem was O'Grady, of course. But there was another one. Halloran or no, we had a real rat inside AXE. Somebody had sold us out, and funneled secrets to them, and . . . .

"Right," I said. "We've got work to do."

We walked away from the phone kiosk just in time to run into the delivery man bringing in fresh copies of the latest edition of the *Atlanta Journal.*

Sinead spotted them first. My own glance was more than a moment behind hers. The large-size type was glaring; bold black letters asking ominously, END OF THE WORLD?

The little kicker up in the corner said *"Doomsday Threat"* and also clear as hell was a four-column cut of a dull gray ball which I'd have given fifty-to-one odds was the planet Mars.

I whistled.

"Jesus," Sinead said. For some reason when Irish Catholics take the name of the Lord in vain they manage to make it sound like music. She went over and bought one of the first copies. It was fresh enough off the presses to dirty your hands when you picked it up.

We sat down to read it. There wasn't much that we both didn't know already. But the cards were out on the table now. And the stakes had just gone up enormously.

For one thing, in addition to the usual hassle, and the three-day deadline, there'd be the panic in New York. I put the paper down after getting the message—the *Journal* had replated for the story and printed it without jumps—and let my breath out slow, through my mouth.

"Yes," she said. "My God."

I was sitting there thinking, my mind running like forty and my heart pounding in time with it, when the PA system broke into my consciousness: *"Paging Mr. Bender. Paging Mr. Clarence Bender. . . ."*

"Hey," Sinead said to my retreating back. "Nick, where . . . ." But I was gone. I made it to the desk on the dead run, leaving her to figure out what was happening and tag along. The guy at the desk showed me to a bank of phones. I picked up the one on the end and punched a button, "Bender here."

"Sixty-forty."

"Hike."

"Okay. I thought I'd be able to get you." Hawk's voice was tight and controlled. "Cancel your ticket and get one for New York. No, make that two. I'll need both of you. You ought to be able to make it into town from Kennedy—"

"No." I thought a moment and then I said, "Sir."

"What the hell do you mean no?" Hawk said. I was sure he'd bit through his cigar by now. "Orders, Nick."

"I'm declining them. I'm heading for D.C."

"The hell you are. You're . . . ."

"Look, you've got everything as much under

control in New York as it's going to get right now. I don't have any New York ideas that you haven't already thought of. I'll put Sinead on the plane to Kennedy. Me, I'm going back to D.C. We have two problems, not one, if you remember."

Hawk thought a moment on that one. He let his breath out. "Maybe you're right. Send the Irish girl along, though. She seems to be all right."

"She's more than all right and you know it. And so is the Mulrae kid."

"But Nick—what do you think you're going to do?"

"You know damn good and well what I'm going to do."

He thought about that for a moment, too. "Yes, I do," he said. "And you're right. But get the hell up here to Fun City the minute you're free."

"That'll be as quick as I can make it. See you soon," I said. Then I thought of something. "Who the hell was our agent in Hong Kong twenty years ago? The one with the funny handshake?" I asked him.

"The one Kurt Schindler murdered? Will Lockwood. You know that. What the hell . . . ."

"See you in New York, boss," I said, and I hung up.

I put Sinead on the plane, and when I kissed her goodbye her eyes were soft and warm and her lips were full of a delicate and subtle yielding. "Take care," she whispered, and then she walked down the ramp to the big L-1011. I didn't wait for takeoff. I had a plane of my own to catch. And strangely enough, I felt good about my job for the first time in days.

An hour or two and there I was, coming up Connecticut Avenue and going around the circle to pull up right down the street from Bialek's bookstore. And who should I run into, coming out of the cafeteria on the corner, but Bob Franks.

"Nick," he said. "Say, you came along at just the right time. Where's the forty bucks you owe me? The landlord is putting up a hell of a fuss about that building I rented for the Baroque Dance group. If I don't stick some dough in his fist by this afternoon he's going to . . . ."

I grabbed him by the coat and shoved him into a doorway. Inside the building I hustled him along by the collar and the seat of the pants until we were inside the men's john. I kicked open all the stalls, making sure nobody was there, holding him by the scruff and the ass the whole time.

"Hey," he said. "We've got to stop meeting like this. People will say we're in love. I knew you'd turn fruit. You're the type. I knew it all along . . . ."

"Shut up," I said. "What's the chord progression for the *passamezzo moderno*?"

"Huh?" he looked at me blankly. I shook him a little harder. "Okay, damn it. 1-1-4-4-1-1-5-5-1-1-4-4-1-5-1-1. That's roman numerals, mind you. The *passamezzo moderno* is a ground bass pattern which first appears around 1505. It later comes to be called the Quadro Pavane, *Les Bouffons,* and Gregory Walker. Go out in the sticks and you'll find it being played in square-dance bands as *Bile Them Cabbage Down.* You dance it by . . . ."

I let him go. "That's okay," I said. "Sorry. I had to make sure you were yourself. Everybody and his goddamn brother is turning out to be somebody else these days. How the hell did you know I was alive? You didn't do a double take. Everybody's supposed to think I'm dead."

"Yeah. I went to your funeral. Hey, you owe me ten bucks more for flowers. Anyhow, I figured if you were dead you were dead. If you turned back up again it was okay for me to act normal. Hawk clued me in a while back. Why, was I supposed to cut you dead? Make like I didn't know you?"

"No," I said. "You're right on the ball. Just keep doing what you were doing." I pulled out my wallet and checked my dough. "Look, I only have a twenty."

Franks grabbed the bill, then asked, "Where are you going?"

"Upstairs. Want to tag along?"

"Sure. What's up?"

"You watch." I headed for the stairs. He stayed with me, but I could hear him puffing. The derring-do really wasn't in his line, but he was game for anything. He'd do. I'd decided that quite a little while ago.

In front of the Amalgamated Press and Wire Services office I took a deep breath. "Stand back," I said. Franks—his reflexes were pretty quick, all in all—stepped back into the hall.

I kicked in the door.

David Hawk sat there, the usual sort of disreputable cigar in his mouth. "Nick," he said in that sour voice of his. "What the hell are you doing here? You're supposed to . . . ."

Wilhelmina was in my hand. I didn't stop to think. I shot him once between the eyes.

The middle of David Hawk's face collapsed totally, in a red mass of blood. A gray-and-red mess of brains came out of the back of his head and painted the rear wall. The body slumped forward. David Hawk was dead.

"Hey," Bob Franks said behind me. He leaned back against the wall. And, little by little, he let his breath out.

"Come in," I said. And I moved forward to yank that ruined face back into view again, holding on by the sparse topknot on Hawk's head.

The hair came off in my hand. Phony, of course.

I looked around. Franks stood in the door. His eyes went to the mess I'd been holding in my hand, and then back to my face, and then to the body again. He gulped loudly. Then he blew again, and managed some kind of a smile.

"It isn't Hawk," he said.

"No," I said. I shoved Wilhelmina back in her holster. "I don't know exactly who he is; the other day he sat in for Hawk on the international wire and steered me into a trap halfway around the world. He . . . ."

"Hey," Franks said. "You just turned white as a sheet."

I was remembering the conversation. "God dammit, he's got Mamie Allen."

"No he hasn't," Franks said.

"How the hell do you know?" I said. "I tell you, I blabbed about Mamie the other day. This guy was sitting in for Hawk. He'd know all about her. He'd be waiting for her when she got into town. He. . . ."

"No he wouldn't. Hawk—I guess it must have been the right one, not this bird—got in touch with me and asked me for a good place to stash her for a few days. As it happened I knew a place."

"Where?" I said.

"Out at the Renaissance Fair, in Poolesville. Where else? The annual blowout of the Miniver Cheevy Society, founded by Your Humble Servant four years ago and dedicated to the proposition that the time is out of joint and it's about time somebody put it right . . . ."

"Renaissance Fair?"

"Yeah. Mamie turned out to be the best damn contralto anybody's sent us in a month of Sundays. Reads music like nobody's business, and that nice golden skin looks smashing in those pastel robes . . ."

"Hey," I said. "Who else knows about this? Mamie, I mean?"

"Oh," he said. "Nobody outside AXE. Nick,

it's okay, really. She's safe as . . . ."

"She isn't safe at all," I said. "Look, we've got to get out there right now. Come on."

"Hey," Franks said. "Aren't we going to clean up the mess?" He gestured, with a mild wince, at the body.

"No time," I said. "I know a number to call. Sort of a federal janitorial service. By the time we're back the joint will be in apple-pie order. Meanwhile, let's get moving. Usually Mamie can take care of herself. But it isn't small-stakes stuff any more, and believe me, pal, she's in worse trouble right now than she ever got into in Mississippi."

Franks gulped. Then he gave me that lopsided grin of his. It looked sheepish rather than confident. "I sure hope you know what you're doing."

"That makes two of us," I said. "Come on. I just hope we aren't too late."

FIFTEEN

THE GARAGE WOULDN'T let me have my car. It was tied up in probate or something since I'd forgotten to write a will. No matter. I hit the Hertz office and scored a big heavy gas-guzzler of a Mercury, fast and powerful, a four-flusher's car.

We needed something fast, and something that cornered nicely on bum roads. Highway 28 was still the best way to Poolesville short of a helicopter, and while I ordinarily had no objections to one of those, this time it'd have flushed our prey—and likely put Mamie's life in even greater danger.

Poolesville is a sleepy little burg, population maybe 300, and while it's no more than twenty miles from the D.C. line, somehow the world has passed it by. There isn't a freeway nearby; there isn't even a bridge across the Potomac to Leesburg, the nearest town. You have to take the car ferry.

Beside me on the seat Bob Franks was raising a sweat as I skidded around a curve, skirting somebody's cornfield, at sixty-five. "Patience," I said. "You couldn't be safer in your mother's pram."

"It's nothing," he said through clenched teeth. "I just thought I felt us touch the ground once or twice back there." I shot him a glance. He was climbing into the shoulderbelt, and he was chewing on that sandy mustache of his again.

"I'm curious," I said. "Why Poolesville?"

"Because it's cheap. It's the best we can do until the Rockefeller Foundation decides to start footing the bills. Lately the government has been very antsy on the question of what they're going to pay the farmers out this way not to grow. It behooves Foxy Grandpa in his bib overalls to find some steady use of his pasture."

"So he lets you put up your stalls and pitch your tents for a song. Why a Renaissance Fair, though?"

"I got jilted some years ago by a girl who played the recorder. Out of a sense of loss and sheer tenacity to show her, I learned the instrument. Next thing you know I was up to my eyes in old-music buffs. That led to deciding we ought to look like the music we were playing. Then came banners flying overhead, and a medieval feast, with everybody eating off trenchers. Then we started learning the dances, and that led to learning how to cold-cock each other with 15th century weapons, or brew mead, or sew sequins on a cod-piece . . . ."

"Sort of a controlled fantasy, huh?"

"Yeah. Our way you can pick your own version of reality and leave out the part that stinks. There are times when I wish I could do that with the 1970s."

"Point well taken," I agreed, thinking there was a lot I'd like to have left out of the present caper.

"Here," he said. "Ignore the signs. Take the dirt road. That'll bring you out behind the fair. Shortcut. And you stand a better chance of sneaking up on somebody this way."

"Okay," I said. And nearly shook the teeth out of his head making the turn at full speed in a controlled skid. About a hundred yards down the road I could see the gaily colored banners flying and I slowed down.

When we pulled to a halt Franks said, "Hey. I was looking for the red light to go on and tell me I could smoke. And whatever happened to the stewardess who's supposed to come through with the cold TV dinners and the watery highballs?"

"Come on," I said. "I see a hole in the fence."

The Renaissance Fair, Miniver Cheevy Society

style, smelled of cowshit and marijuana. The big surprise, though, wasn't how many teen-agers and under-thirties you saw out there strutting around in tights or heavy skirts. It was the forties and fifties—professional people, folks who dressed conservatively out there in the world and minded their manners and kept up with the Joneses. As we walked down the field amid the gay banners, listening to the pipes blasting away and the out-of-tune shawms and sackbuts honking nearby, a lady passed us on a gorgeously draped horse. Her outfit was something to see. Of course she cut us dead, baseborn scum that we were.

"That one was modeled after Chaucer's Wife of Bath," Bob said, puffing along beside me. "Remember English Lit 101:

> Hir coverchiefs ful fyne were of ground;
> I dorste swere they weyeden ten pound
> That on a Sonday were upon hir heed . . . .
> Upon an amblere esily she sat,
> Y-wimpled wel, and on hir heed an hat
> As brood as is a bokeler or a targe . . . ."

"Bob," I said, stepping out of the way of a motley acrobat doing cartwheels to the rhythm of a tambourine, "is there anything you don't know?"

"Yeah," Franks said ruefully. "How to get rich." His tone changed. "Hey, Nick," he said. "There she is. The madrigal singers, right over there on the platform."

"Right," I said. She looked gorgeous just as he'd said she would. There were four of them, two women and two men, and the robes were four different pastel colors. They were singing something soft and lovely about a silver swan, singing its last song before it died.

I scanned the crowd. I wasn't sure just what the hell to look for. I couldn't recognize these guys in normal street clothes, much less in the sleeveless jerkins and tights that were the order of the day here. "Bob," I said. "Soon as the song's over slip up there and tell them to knock it off. And get Mamie back under cover somewhere. Maybe the big tent. Here, you'll need this. Don't let anybody get close to her." I pitched Wilhelmina to him. He caught her and stuffed her in a pocket. He nodded gamely and burrowed into the crowd before the singers' platform like a stubborn little redheaded mole. I turned and ran into somebody, hard.

It was a woman in one of those outfits, and when I knocked her over the ensemble needed some untangling. But when I managed to get her out from under those crumpled folds of cloth and sit her up on the ground beside me, damned if I didn't know her.

"Sally!" I said. "Sally Scharff!"

Her hand went to her mouth, and all the color left her face. She almost fainted right there. I could tell from the first sight of her that she wasn't well. I hadn't seen her in about six months—she ran the switchboard downstairs from David Hawk's place—and she'd gone downhill terribly since then. She'd been pretty once, and in her mid-thirties or so she still ought to be.

Then I thought about it. Damn! She'd thought I was dead. "Sally," I said. "It's Nick. I'm back. Are you okay?"

Her eyes fluttered; then, getting it back together, she tried to smile. "Nick . . . thank God . . . I have to talk to you . . . please." She grabbed my hand. There wasn't any more strength in her squeeze than there'd be in a baby's. "Nick . . . it's urgent. Take me out of here, please . . . over there. . . ." She pointed to a shady spot under the trees.

"Can you walk?" I said. "I'll get you up slowly if you're dizzy. You . . . ." But it didn't look like she could. And when she tried, holding on to my arm, she went right out of it. Clean passed out.

I looked around. Nobody seemed to be paying much attention to us. I decided to take her up on that suggestion about getting her out of the line of fire. When I stood her up, all dead weight the way she was, she still wasn't heavy. What in God's name had happened to her?

There turned out to be a way I could grab her under the arms, from the back, that looked like I was dancing with her. The stiff collar of her gown held her neck nice and high, and when I pulled the hood down over her eyes she looked like somebody who was awake, perhaps—but with her mouth lolling open like that I'd have to hope people would think she had asthma. As the mummers plowed through the crowd, heading our way and banging on that tambourine again, I took the opportunity to trip the light fantastic with her over to that handy grove of trees on the edge of the hill.

I got over the hill into a pleasant little dale among the spreading apple trees and sat her up against one. I rubbed some circulation back into her hands and presently she was looking at me again, the color coming back into her face little by little.

Then she remembered. "Nick! Oh, Nick, I'm so glad you're here . . . things have gone so awfully wrong . . . I've been such a fool . . . ."

"What's the matter, Sally?"

"Nick, I—I've sold you out. I've made such a mess of things . . . ."

"What do you mean, honey? How could you sell us out? What do you . . ."

"No, Nick." Her hand was on mine again, and the look in her eyes was full of pain. "No, it's for real. They told me at first that nobody'd come to harm. That it was just a matter of the citizen's right to keep tabs on government. They were just going to put a couple of taps on your phone system . . . ."

"Oh," I said. "That's okay. They were the good guys. We found the bugs, anyhow." But as I looked in her eyes I remembered. And the look on her face would have told me anyhow.

"I—I don't know these people. I mean Mack. And O'Grady, and . . . ."

"Sally!" I said. "What are you saying? Where's Mack? And what did they talk you into doing?" I had my hands on her upper arms, ready to start shaking her. Then I saw the blue cast to her features, and knew something was wrong. Dead wrong.

"I . . . that's all right, Nick, I think . . . I think I won't last much longer . . . . the doctors told me . . . they told me . . . three months . . . it's been six . . . and . . . and Mack was so sweet to me . . . it was going to be my last little love affair, you know . . . and he was so gentle and loving and caring at first. . . ."

"Mack?" I said. "Mack Halloran? He got you to let the guys into the phone complex? To set up the equipment, to patch in on our communications?"

"Nick . . . yes . . . he's here . . . the black girl . . . he'll kill her . . . Mr. Hawk mentioned where they were taking her on the phone . . . we caught this . . . Mack did, anyway . . . he brought me out here. . . ."

"Jesus Christ," I said. "Sally, what does he look like? Is he in costume? How do I recognize him?"

She started to tell me something. Then the life just sort of slipped away from her in one big rush, taking her breath with it. The light died in her eyes. He mouth closed. The hand on mine went limp. I pinched it. No feeling. Then I tried her pulse. Nothing.

I got up, feeling sour. Across the hill the madrigalists ended their song about the dying swan. The words came softly and clearly to my ear: *Farewell all joys! O death come close my eyes; More geese than swans now live, more fools than wise . . . .*

Mamie! She was still there, and singing! I must have given a little start at the thought. Some sort of little nervous tic. I shook my head to one side . . . and a damned good thing too. The heavy blade came whizzing by me at a hell of a clip. It made a *swooshing* sort of sound. I ducked, hit the ground, rolled, and came up with my feet under me, ten feet from where I'd stood.

And whirled to have a look at him.

Whoever he was, he was big. I couldn't make out much more than that. He wore a suit of chain mail with a hood and a pointed Viking helmet on top of it. This had a broad nosepiece that hung way down over his face. I couldn't pick his features out of all that to save me.

Frankly, I wasn't trying. The thing he had in his hands, the thing he'd damn near killed me with, was occupying all of my attention.

It was a sort of glorified headsman's axe, broad, heavy and sharp, on an eight or ten-foot pole. He was swinging it around and around his head, and it was coming closer to me with every step he took, slow and deliberate. I moved away cautiously, keeping my eyes on his hands, wishing I could make out his eyes under that hood . . . then I tripped on something and fell flat on my back.

The halberd went past my face like something shot out of a gun. I rolled. He stepped forward, swinging again; this time the blade can't have missed me by more than an inch or two.

I rolled again, once, twice. I gave a twist to it and tumbled to one side. It was the saving of me. The next swing of the blade had too much momentum behind it—a heavy axe blade like that has a devil of a lot of inertia—for him to change directions on it. And turning to face me in my new position put him off his steady forward stride.

It was just enough.

I rushed him. And this time I got inside of the swing. The blade couldn't touch me this way. The handle could, though, and when it caught me amidships it brought me to my knees—and the halberd went flying out of his hand.

I shook Hugo out of my sleeve and into my palm.

He reached for a dagger at his waist, but not quickly enough. I lunged forward on my knees and jabbed him in the thigh, hard.

He swore and staggered back. I'd hit something important; the leg wouldn't work right. I got my feet under me and rushed him. He got that good leg behind him and parried my first lunge; the dagger in his hand then cut over the point and went for my neck. I backed off and nicked his arm with Hugo, right through the mail, right above the heavy gauntlet he wore. It hurt him; he almost dropped the knife. But then he switched hands and came after me. Dark blood dripped from the chain links on that wounded arm, and his limp was worse than it had been.

I backed away again and ran into a low-lying limb of the apple tree. It nearly knocked me silly. As I shook my head he was upon me. The dagger went for my face, and I barely got out of the way in time; he sliced a slit down my cheek. I threw up one hand, the one with Hugo in it, to fend him off and he ran right onto it. That funny helmet had spaces beside the nosepiece for the eyes. Hugo just slipped in and took out his right eye, and went all the way in until he hit bone.

The knight dropped on his face. He convulsed once, twice . . . and then it was all over for him.

I stepped back, breathing hard and reached down, gingerly, with the point of Hugo to pry that Viking helmet off.

It was Mack Halloran, all right. I reached down with Hugo again, even more carefully this time, and pulled the gauntlet off that awful hand, the one I'd seen in the videotape in Sydney.

There wasn't anything wrong with him at all. Other than the fact that he was dead.

I hauled him back in the bushes and covered him up. Then, on impulse, I moved Sally to the same place. No use in sticking around to talk to the cops. Not with a deadline like the one *we* had to deal with. And, with one last glance back at them, I took off for the other side of the hill where Bob Franks was shepherding Mamie Allen across the meadow. When they caught sight of me Franks breathed an audible sigh . . . and Mamie broke into a broad grin. "Nick!" she said. I let her run right into my arms, and she felt damn good.

Franks's apprehensive eyes flickered back and forth under those sandy brows. "Nick . . . you're sure they're not . . . ."

I held out my hand for Wilhelmina and he unobtrusively dropped the gun in my palm. "Pal, I'm not sure of anything," I said. "Let's get out of here before I really get paranoid."

I sounded confident. I usually do. I have a way of making even a doubtful statement like that one sound as though I didn't mean a word of it. End of the world? All in the day's work. Doomsday Spore? Duck soup.

Don't believe a word of it. *I* sure as hell didn't.

SIXTEEN

IT'S ALMOST IMPOSSIBLE to describe what the scene was like trying to get into New York. The tunnels and bridges were clogged with people on foot, trying to get off Manhattan, carrying suitcases, children, pets. That was the first full day of it, when the police had given up and the National Guard hadn't arrived yet. Under the circumstances martial law didn't mean a damn thing.

I know they played it down afterward. The networks allowed only selected footage through, and that was calculated to reassure. Everything was set up to make viewers feel good, to make sure nobody got hurt in the panic. The people who did, in fact, get hurt somehow managed to stay out of the statistics. Instead of riots and panic, what was seen on the six o'clock news was the chief of police emphasizing he had everything under control. Of course martial law had been declared, but the only thing that got taken over was the press. Outside, where the cops couldn't do a damn thing about the crowds, it was a madhouse.

But the bulk of the nation will never see film footage of the hundreds of thousands pouring out of the Holland Tunnel and jamming the George Washington Bridge. Federal inspectors destroyed it all.

It was an impossible situation. A human sea of terrified people, uncontrollable millions, blocking all main streets, exits . . . As it was I took the Pennsy as far as Elizabeth, New Jersey. There it stopped. Everybody off. You couldn't get a train on that damn tunnel; it was clogged with pedestrians going both ways. Same with the Staten Island ferry from St. George; once the boats made it, overloaded like that, from the Battery pilots all went on strike and wouldn't take the ferries back the other way. Coming in from Kennedy would have been even worse.

In retrospect, I think I did the right thing. Which was to pop out to the Newark airport, right down the road, and flash the credentials that got me a copter. We went across the Hudson, looking down at the lemmings in their mad dash for safety, and put down on top of the Pan Am building.

Thank God *everybody* hadn't given up. The elevator staff at the Pan Am hadn't, for instance. The funny thing was, there was still a lot of business going on more or less as usual up at the stratosphere level, all around midtown. You could look around from the heliport area and see windows lit, and people going about their business, in the Chrysler Building and the two big black towers of the World Trade Center. If you kept your eyes on the top of New York, now, you'd think it was a more or less normal day—perhaps, from the number of offices that didn't have lights on in them, a Jewish holiday or something.

The elevator operator had a disappointed look on his face when he answered a heliport call and found out it wasn't the U.S. Cavalry or the Airborne coming in to save the world. Just me, in my bureaucrat suit. I'd stashed Bob and Mamie with some government folks for the duration and come up by myself. Sinead had some reporting and conferring to do at her Embassy, and I'd left her with them.

I smiled back at the elevator man. "Uh, fine day. Uh, for a helicopter ride anyhow."

"Are you kidding?" he said. "What are you doing coming into the city? Everybody wants to get out."

"Uh, yes. Well, I'm a big butter and egg man

from Dubuque. Business has to go on despite adversity, come war and plague and pestilence and famine and destruction. Neither rain nor snow nor dark of night shall stay these hens from the swift completion of their appointed eggs."

"Horseshit." His expression was standard New York Sour, maybe eight on a scale of ten. "You sure you want to get off down there at street level?"

"You tell me. What's the lobby like?"

"A nuthouse. You remember this is right next to Grand Central and the IRT transfer point. And no matter how lousy it gets above ground, don't go down those goddamn subway stairs, pal. It's worse down there than anything you could possibly imagine." He pursed his lips and blew.

"The TV says things are under control here."

"The TV says you can get laid by Miss America if you use the right after-shave. Things ain't gonna begin to get under control until the army comes in. And they're gonna have to mow down a few thousand people on the bridges to get here. You saw what it was like."

"Well, I'm sure Uncle Sam is on the job. You'd be surprised." He would, too. Things were even worse than he thought they were.

Some city services were still working, after a fashion. It made me feel good to know the telephone company was on the job. At the moment it was the only way to get David Hawk. In the lobby things had cooled off a bit—after all, nobody was coming into the Pan Am now since the hand-lettered sign went up on the door saying copter service had been discontinued. I went over to the phone rack and called in.

"Yeah?" The voice was unmistakable. I should have caught the phony Hawk the day of the Sydney call just on nuance alone. Eight thousand miles away, though, it was a lousy connection, and . . . . Well, so was this one, but this time I knew who I was talking to all right.

"Sixty-forty," I said.

"Hike. Where've you been?"

"I've been busy bumping you off. And then I. . . ."

"What do you mean?"

"The CIA janitorial squad ought to be peeling you off the floor at Amalgamated right about now."

"What's happened?

"They got to the switchboard girl. Remember Sally?"

"The one that looks like she's got something."

"Yeah. She did have something. Halloran *was* one of the bad guys. Sorry, boss. First the bad news, then the good. Anyhow, he conned her into letting him and O'Grady bollix up the phone lines in the building. They not only had taps on, they had a patch-in whenever you were out of the office. Then when you took off for New York they moved another guy that looked just like you into the office."

"Okay." The voice was sour as hell. "That's the bad news. What's the good?"

"Well, I got Halloran. And either that wasn't him on the videotape they showed me in Sydney, or . . . . he was faking it. Anyhow, he wasn't wearing any of that gray stuff. He . . . ."

"Nick!" Hawk's voice had a new energy in it. "Get the hell up here right now. Right now. On the double."

"Okay," I said. "Where's here?"

"Room 405, Empire State Building."

"Be there as soon as I can." I hung up and went out the front door. My foot hit the street; the excrement hit the air circulator. It was as close to simultaneous as you can get. Right outside the door three guys were mugging a fourth, or trying to. He was putting up a nice fight of it. Two of them were holding him, or doing their damndest to, and the other was trying to slug him.

Well, I thought, time for a good deed. I clipped the puncher on the ear with a nice straight right and he went down. The guy they were using for a punching bag struggled one arm free and creamed the man who'd been holding him on the left. I spun the other man loose and heaved him through a plate glass window. It made a nice satisfying crash. The window was maybe ten by fifteen feet.

I looked at the guy I'd helped out; he didn't seem hurt. Then we both looked at the window.

"Not to worry," he smiled. "I'm a cop. And, thanks."

I set off down the middle of 43rd St, at a comfortable pace, the sort of thing you'd use if you were going for the Olympic 10,000 meters. Up ahead there were a couple of fires and some kids were carrying televisions out of a broken window. I wondered just what the hell they were going to do with them, and whether they'd given that part of the deal any thought so far. You sure as hell couldn't sell 'em on the Island, and how were you going to get 'em out of town right now? The one thing you see damn little of during a stress situation is evidence of human intelligence.

I stopped a moment at Fifth to get my bearings, and then set out again, this time turning south. The pace stayed easy. I passed people heading the same direction, carrying suitcases, shopping bags. One guy was carrying what looked like a .410 gauge shotgun, and another fellow had a pearl-handled revolver strapped to his side. Well, I couldn't say I blamed them. I'd have felt a little odd without Wilhelmina right then myself.

And then up ahead somebody coming out of a building on the Avenue—a guy with a briefcase and a vested suit, he looked like an investment broker or something with his gray hat and silver hair—saw me, did a take and started to run.

Almost as if he knew me. And didn't want to.

Well, I thought, stranger things have happened. Life is coincidence, after all. I didn't know who the hell he was, but he seemed to know me. I picked up the pace a little and went after him.

He looked around once and saw me behind him. He dropped the briefcase then and turned on the steam. At Forty-Second he turned right and kept going. Well, it was out of my way, but . . . . I broke stride for a moment, thinking of Hawk. Then I turned the corner and went after him.

He was in good shape. The little bit of lead I'd given him, added to the break I'd given him when I hesitated, was going to make him a hard man to catch. It didn't help any when a crowd of kids in black leather jackets tried to bar my way and I had to cream two of them to get free. By the time I'd got back into my jogging pace I could see up ahead that he had two-thirds of a block lead on me and he wasn't about to slow down. Once, he craned his neck around and saw me on his heels still. Then he put his head down and really started to hoof it.

Up ahead at Sixth Avenue another roving gang, heading south, cut him off from me. They looked like trouble this time; they saw me coming and fanned out, linking hands, to bar my way. I had a good look at a couple of faces. They looked like timberwolves hungry for blood. "Damn," I said, and slowed to a trot as I yanked Wilhelmina out of her holster. I drew a bead on the guy in the middle and went straight for him. Then I squeezed one round off, aiming at a close miss, hoping to break his confidence and open a hole in that deadly line. He picked exactly the wrong time to flinch. The big 9mm slug caught him in the shoulder and knocked him over. The guys on both sides of him spun away, alarmed. I went through that hole like Namath, picking the pace back up again.

Halfway up the block I stopped dead. Just for safety's sake I shot a quick glance back at the kids on the street; they'd decided against following me, and I was damn glad of that.

I was, half a block from Seventh Avenue, and there wasn't a sign of the guy I'd been chasing anywhere. And while the corners behind me had been full of people, Times Square, up ahead where Broadway crossed Seventh, was all but empty. The reason? All those cop helicopters cruising the area. Times Square is nice and open, and no particular hazard to the whirlies. They were keeping that one area of Manhattan clean, and the hell with the rest.

I stood there, hands on hips, wondering how I had lost him. Where the hell had he gone? If I had to get out of the way in a hurry in this neighborhood, where would I go?

The answer was right in front of my eyes. I'd go *down!* Down the stairs into that handy subway kiosk. And I could disappear there about as well as I could disappear anywhere in New York.

I stuffed Wilhelmina away in her holster and took the stairs two at a time, entering a different world.

There are two parts of Manhattan that are very probably unique in the world. They're the part that's more than 50 stories high (just try naming a dozen cities with buildings that tall) and the part that begins when you go down those steps into Rapid Transit Land. All the other undergrounds of the world are nothing at all like this one that connects Van Cortlandt Park and the South Ferry, that connects the Village with Brooklyn, that ties midtown Manhattan and the Bronx and Pelham Bay and Queens and Jamaica all together in one big sprawling mess of underground spaghetti. The London underground is more efficient (and safer in wartime). The Moscow subway is incomparably more elegant, and the BART in the Bay Area, out West, is newer and cleaner. The only one that I know of that's even remotely like the New York one is the Paris Metro, and even that has something of the character of that square, pleasant city. The New York subway, though? It's like nothing else.

And, of course, the strangest, most alien part of it is that corridor I'd entered—the one that runs under Seventh Avenue from 34th Street to 42nd Street. There, for some reason, you can walk directly, without passing through a single turnstile, for eight blocks under the city streets. You can pass fast-food joints, newsstands, novelty stores. You can get your hair cut and your shoes shined. You can get raped, mugged, rolled, propositioned by prostitutes . . . .

Well, that's the way it is usually.

Now it was a jungle. An honest to God jungle.

I hadn't gone twelve steps, moving down the long row of darkened shops, before I heard the footsteps behind me. I wheeled. Four dudes in Superfly outfits moved silently into place, cutting me off from the street.

I wheeled again. And there were four more on the other side, and this crowd was Latino and, unlike the knife-wielding black dudes, they were armed with bike chains. I've never seen so many gold teeth in so many unfriendly smiles in my whole life.

And now there were the voices:

"*Hey, man . . . hey, man, come here . . . less boogie . . . .*"

" *. . . Venga aca, chingao . . . .*"

Well, Carter, I was telling myself, you gotta admit Hawk told you to come straight there and not take any side trips. Seems he knew what he was talking about.

SEVENTEEN

UP AHEAD, BEHIND the four Latinos, there was a quick movement in the shadows. Then out of a dark storefront I saw the guy in the suit make his own break for it. How he'd got past these guys in the first place I had no idea, but there he was . . . and he was getting away again.

That made up my mind for me. If I fought my way back through the black dudes I'd find myself on the street, but if I could open a hole in that line ahead of me I might stand a chance of catching the guy I'd been chasing all those blocks. Well, I thought, you've invested this much time and sweat in him, you might as well finish what you started out to do.

I rushed them.

The first bicycle chain snaked out, aimed at my face. I ducked under it and, reaching up from below, grabbed it close to where it was wrapped around the kid's hand. I yanked, hard as hell, and dove at his middle. He went up and over my back on the ground. I heard a scream of pain from him, a scream that knew no language.

That put me right in the middle of them. Out came Hugo; his razor-sharp edge ran along the forearm of one of them, bringing a freshet of blood from an opened vein. He cursed. The guy behind me jumped me; the arm around my neck got another taste of Hugo as I ripped up from below at his wrist with the shiny blade. Simultaneously I butted him hard in the face with my head. The grip relaxed. I took the occasion to shove Hugo up to the hilt in the guy who was rushing me from the front. He dropped, holding his gut. The fourth one took one look at the three of them and ran—straight onto the knives of the four blacks.

I didn't even look around. I hightailed it—down that chiaroscuro corridor. Thank God, I told myself, for the echo. If I hadn't got some help from the crazy acoustics down there—the kind that let you know, half a block away, that you've just missed your train—I couldn't have kept up with the sound of the man ahead of me. As it was I could hear the amplified sound of his feet pounding up ahead mainly because I stayed out of step with him. I could hear his footfalls sandwiched between mine.

Then all of a sudden I couldn't hear them at all.

I stopped and looked around. Who knew what was happening in the shadows?

Nothing behind me, so far as I could see. Up ahead . . . .

Damn! I'd thought he was heading, say, for the Macy's exit. There were, however, a couple of subsidiary entrance kiosks stationed between the two main outlets, although offhand I couldn't remember what street they let out at.

He'd had perhaps a hundred yards headstart on me. There weren't that many places to disappear into. And whatever happened, he wasn't running now. I could walk down the way, keeping my eyes and ears open, and take my time . . . as much time, anyhow, as the general conditions down there called for or would allow.

It was about time to yank out Wilhelmina again. And, given the circumstances, I wished I had a spare magazine around somewhere. Worse: I wished the old girl had one of those 32-shot snail magazines they developed around World War I to convert weapons like Wilhelmina into submachine guns. I had a feeling that an adaptor like that would be coming in handy before this case was over.

I almost walked right past him—the guy in the

gray suit. Something told me to shoot a glance at that shadowed doorway, though, and it probably saved my skin. When I did look, he had an ugly old Webley .455 automatic pointed at my gut.

"Drop it," he said. "The gun, Carter."

I made a move to toss Wilhelmina . . . but I went with her. And hit. And rolled. And wound up behind a metal trashcan. The Webley went off—deafeningly, four times—and drilled three holes in the can right where I'd have been if I hadn't rolled to the ground and flattened myself on my belly. The Webley has a hell of a lot of hitting power, and that old collector's item shoots a damn sight straighter than our old .45.

I reached around the can and squeezed off a round in his direction, not hoping to hit anything so much as to drive him back into cover and let me get into a better position. This brought on two more shots.

I snuck back behind an iron stanchion. Six shots. If I kept him too busy to reload that meant he had only two shots left; the Webley holds one in the chamber and seven in the clip. I was thinking. . . .

"Hey!" I said. "Let's make a deal. I don't know you. All I know is who you work for." Carter, what a bluff. You don't know a damn thing about him and you know it.

"Deal?" he said. "What kind of deal?"

"Sell me O'Grady and you can disappear right now and nobody'll follow you. Until you get in our hair again, anyhow."

"Aren't you displaying a lot of confidence in what is actually an inferior situation? After all, we have the upper hand. Surely you must have looked around you, back on the surface. New York is a madhouse. Everyone in the city, by now, must know of what we have threatened to do if our demands are not met."

"Yeah?" I said. I hoped I could pull it off. "Well, they don't know you bunch of phonies. They think you're on the level. I know better."

"Know better? What do you mean?"

"Come on, cut the malarkey. I just got here, my friend. I was in D.C. breaking up that end of your operation. I got the man who was impersonating David Hawk. I . . . ."

"What?" That caught him off balance.

"You heard me. And we've broken up the phone bug and all the rest. Sally Scharff is dead. So is Mack Halloran." I heard his quick intake of breath and plowed onward. "Yeah. I killed the son of a bitch myself. We're compromised, of course. Our whole old network is broken, out in the clear. What Mack didn't know and couldn't tell you, however, is that we've got a whole new set of systems, ready to switch to them in case of compromises. We're already patched into them. You've got our setup all right. But it's dead. We're already working on the new one. And Mack didn't know a thing about that."

"No matter, Carter. We've still got the weapon that can stop you. If our demands aren't met . . . ."

I pushed on, hard. "You forget. I said *I* got

Halloran. Remember the funny little closed-circuit TV show O'Grady worked up about Halloran? About how he'd been infected by the Spore?"

"I was there. I was 'Alf Beamish.' I recognized you back on the street just now."

"Damn. You could have fooled me. Didn't recognize you at all. But no matter. The main thing is that I know about Halloran, and that funny gray crap that's supposed to have been eating him alive. Pal, it's a phony. There wasn't anything wrong with Halloran at all except that he was a yellow rat who sold us out. True, that turned out to be just as fatal as the gray stuff was supposed to have been, but . . . ."

"Carter. You're bluffing."

"No, I'm not. I checked. What's the matter? You didn't know?" All of a sudden my heart was pounding like crazy. I had indeed been bluffing . . . but it'd worked.

What if the stuff on Halloran was phony—but this guy didn't know it? What if he'd been conned? Which seemed to be the case?

The implications followed thick and fast, but I didn't have time to dwell upon them. It was time for really pressing this guy, backing him to the wall, seeing what I could do with him.

"Carter, if I thought O'Grady had been lying to us . . . ."

"Well, he has, goddammit. Why the surprise. You know he's a double-dealing son of a bitch, don't you? Why should he be straight with you when he lies to everybody else? You think he's in this thing because of the High and Noble Cause? For Irish sovereignty? For independence? Jesus Christ, man, I'm ashamed of you. He's been playing you for a bunch of saps. Can you really believe O'Grady would do anything for any other reason than power?"

"Why should I believe you, Carter?"

"Why shouldn't you? What stake have I got in the matter? I don't give a damn if you take over your island. I also don't care if the limeys come across the channel and shove you all into the sea with bulldozers. Either thing happens, I won't miss a meal."

"Carter . . . ." His voice was tight and phlegmy. He was so worked up he'd be lucky not to pop a blood vessel.

"The really stupid, vicious thing about you guys is that you don't give a damn who it is you kill. Half the time it isn't a limey who opens that letter bomb you send: it's his Irish secretary. You know the Irish girl who works with me? You know why she's working against you? I suppose O'Grady has told you she's sold out to the British, chasing down one of her own people like that. Am I right? Is that the sort of crap he's been feeding you?"

"Go on," he said in a small voice, very self-contained.

"She was Hugh Geoghegan's wife. You know that name. Perhaps O'Grady had reason to hate Geoghegan and wish him out of the way. What did he have against Geoghegan's innocent children? Or anybody else's? Irish children, too, mind you. O'Grady didn't give a damn. When the bomb went off there were thirty of them left dead, all under twelve. To get Geoghegan he was willing to kill thirty innocent children . . . ."

"Carter, get to the point. You're avoiding it. I've had . . . attacks of conscience . . . I can't deny that. . . . But I've always been able to tell myself that the actions were upright ones because the cause was upright, and the cause was upright because Dan was upright. If ever I were to stop believing in Dan. . . ."

"Okay," I edged out to a point where I could look for him there in the shadows. I couldn't make him out yet. "Okay, let's take it one step further. What do you know about the Spore? Is that a phony too?" But when I said it I knew I'd said the wrong thing. I'd taken it just a bit too far. After all, David Hawk had said the Spore was real, that it was missing.

Or had he? I thought back, trying to remember which David Hawk I'd been talking to when I'd heard that about the space lab having some of the stuff missing. But no, it had to be the real one . . . Or did it?

"Carter." His voice was hostile and bitter. "You're bluffing. You're lying. None of it's true, none of it!" Amd he stepped into view and squeezed off another shot at me. He didn't have time to aim. It missed—but came close enough to send me scuttling for cover again.

"Well," I said. "It's showdown time. Either you've got one round left in that magazine, or you're just plain out. But I've only used up two shots. One on you and one on a kid who was trying to mug me. Want to know what the odds on you and me are, pal?"

This time he didn't say anything at all.

Okay, I told myself, it's now or never. I took a deep breath and jumped out into the hall.

The maneuver is what a ballet dancer calls "spotting"—when he does a spin he'll "spot" so that he'll always face the gallery just once, for a split-second, before the spin continues. As I spun out into the corridor I timed my turn so that I'd end facing him in a crouch, both hands on dear old Wilhelmina and her little snub nose pointed right at his chest. It's a bigger target, and if you miss the heart you're sure to hit him someplace where it'll be painful enough.

But he wasn't there at all.

What *was* there was an open door.

I edged forward, wondering where the door led to. When I got close enough to it I knew. I knew by the smell.

The world underneath a great city's streets is a complicated one. It's not just subways down there. There are miles and miles of water lines, phone conduits . . . and the sewer system.

The Department of Sanitation gets down to clear up stoppages in the sewer system at the point where two submains, running ever downward, cross and pass into a main through manholes, characterizied above ground by round, black metal covers. At the bottom of the manhole, open curved channels lead the sewage with a minimum of friction from one pipe into the next, from the smaller pipe to the larger. The overall shape of the manhole itself, as a piece of enclosed space, is something like the shape of one of the masonry beehive tombs the Myceneans used to bury their more notable dead in, four thousand years ago.

There are lots of places where stoppages could occur, and they're not all where it's convenient to put a manhole. There are openings from the subway system. And some damn fool had gone and left one of them unlocked. I held Wilhelmina nice and steady in front of me and edged into the hole in the wall.

At the end of that slowly descending corridor there was a light. I stopped and listened. I could hear moving water. I tiptoed slowly and steadily toward it, listening for any sign of a foreign sound, my eyes on every irregularity in the wall, hoping to God the next step wouldn't see him jumping out from behind something and squeezing off that last round at me.

I stopped dead.

He had had time to reload by now. And I was walking into a trap.

EIGHTEEN

UP AHEAD WHERE the light was coming from I could hear the water splashing. It sounded as though I might come out at a major intersection. I tiptoed forward, pistol at the ready, and came to the door. Taking a deep breath, I stepped through.

The reek was suffocating. The air that far down wasn't all that good anyhow, and added to the general foulness of the place it was pretty overwhelming. I looked around, first up the shaft, then down . . . And found myself staring into the business end of the Webley.

He was standing in the middle of the stream; it was up to his armpits. The Webley was trained on my gut. It was nice and quiet under the roar of the water.

''Drop it,'' he commanded. ''As you may have guessed, Carter, I've reloaded.''

I put Wilhelmina, butt first, gently down on a concrete slab, away from the water.

''Now,'' he said. ''Just stay there while I get out, you . . . .''

Something hit him. Hard.

His head disappeared below the surface. The Webley waved high in the air, then fell from his hands. His head came up; pain showing in his face. ''I . . . . Carter, help!''

I picked up Wilhelmina as I watched him, dumfounded. Whatever had happened happened again. His head jerked violently back under the scummy, foul water. I held the Luger handy, but didn't do anything. And then I saw it. Just one beat of that long saurian tail behind him. About ten or twelve feet behind him . . . .

They're down there after all. And if this one was any indication, they were flourishing on a diet of human waste and garbage. And rats. And dead pets. And people . . . .

A crocodile doesn't come up and tear a chunk off you the way a shark does. His jaws don't move quickly, and he can't roll easily when ripping your flesh away. He has a much simpler method. He just grabs you and sinks to the bottom with you and waits there until you drown. Then he makes a meal out of you at his leisure.

The silver-haired man's head came back up again, and the gasp his mouth made was phlegmy and already full of water. He wasn't getting much air above the waterline, and none at all below. His hand came up as the head went down again, wildly flailing. Then, all of a sudden, it too went limp and slipped below the surface.

Ten feet or so back the big tail thrashed again. Then all was still except the sluggish current, heading down, into the bowels of the earth . . . .

Down the corridor I found a side passage that led to a vaulted area with a patch of light above it: a manhole. I came up again on Fortieth Street just off the exact center of the intersection with Seventh Avenue. Any other time I'd have found myself in the middle of midtown traffic . . . Now the only cars there were cop cars. The police were making a sort of stand of it in the middle of the Island, and apparently the area just below Times Square was headquarters for this. One of them stopped me for a moment, but let me go when I flashed my ID.

I set off at a brisk jog down to Thirty-Fourth Street, just as if nothing had happened. I turned at Macy's and kept going, looking up just once at the stately building that had been the world's tallest before the twin towers of the World Trade Center were erected and the Sears Tower in Chicago had risen above that windy burg. The Empire State Building was still a lovely sight, elegant and graceful without the chunkiness of the World Trade Center slabs or the Art Deco crankiness of the shiny Chrysler tower. Somehow I liked it all the better for the fact that the action had definitely moved to another street corner. I could still see the original King Kong hanging on to the top of it, cold-cocking airplanes with that big fist of his while Fay Wray cringed on a ledge below him.

I jogged up to the door and had to show my credentials to get in. Apparently a building this important still rated city cops of its own. I took the local elevator up to the fourth floor.

I opened 405. It was just like opening the door at Amalgamated. There was David Hawk, the real one, sitting behind a desk, scowling up at me, that awful cigar working in one corner of his mouth, a telephone jammed against his ear. He nodded and went back to his conversation as I closed the door.

"No, sir," Hawk was saying. "We're working on it, but he's got us buffaloed so far. He was supposed to have had a tape loop delivered to the CBS people an hour ago, and they haven't seen hide nor hair of it. Something seems to have gone wrong . . . it looks like the scheduled TV appearance is off . . . and meanwhile we're out of contact with him. We're totally dependent on having him call in. Yes, he's got the number. But he's silent.

Yes, sir. Yes, I realize it's important. But . . . ." He made a sourer-than-usual face. "Yes, *sir.*" He hung up with a bang. Then he looked at me. "Nick. Where the hell have you been? You smell like. . . ."

"Yes sir," I said. "That's where I've been. I take it that was the president?"

"Right. What were you doing down in the sewers?"

"I was chasing . . ." And then it hit me. I think I know where that tape might be. The videotape you were talking about on the phone."

Hawk's eyes were popping. "Where?"

"Fifth Avenue, between Forty-third and Forty-second. Middle of the block. In the gutter on the east side of the street. If somebody hasn't grabbed it by now. Ane there's damn little chance of that. You know what it's like out there."

"Yeah. What happened?"

I told him. "Uh, around 511 or 513. He came out the door there. Two doors from Takashimaya. Hey, damn. Maybe there's still some of them in there. Maybe we should . . . ."

Hawk didn't wait for me to finish. He got on the phone and sent a MASH team down there on the double. Then he turned to me again. "Run the whole story past me again," he said around the cigar.

I tried it again. He sat and listened. "Huh," he said at last. "This guy seemed to be saying that if Halloran's disease—uh, whatever the hell you call that stuff—was phony, it was news to him. Nick, what if the whole thing was phony? After all, all we know for sure is that the stuff is missing from the space lab and they know about it. They could have learned about the missing spore material from the bug on my phone. I've known about that aspect of things for weeks now."

"I've considered that," I said. "I got the strong feeling talking to my little friend back there that I had blown my bluff when I suggested that. Apparently he knew better. Or . . . ."

"Or thought he did, anyway. It's a possibility." His eyes were bright with hope for a moment; then they clouded over again. "We have to expect the worst. It's the only sensible thing to do. I . . . ."

The phone rang.

Hawk looked at me. "Get on the extension over there," he said.

I scuttled over to the other desk. We picked up the phone with a single motion; we'd practiced this one a lot of times before, on other cases.

"David Hawk?" the voice said.

My heart started pounding. I looked at Hawk and nodded. It was him, all right.

"Yeah," Hawk said in his business-as-usual voice.

"This is Daniel O'Grady. No, don't interrupt. Your deadline has been moved back. The man I sent to the television station with the tape was . . . something happened to him. We have reason to suspect that it was your man Carter who stopped

him. The tape never made it to the delivery point.''
I looked at Hawk and nodded. ''My patience is at an end. Therefore, instead of two days, you and your government have . . . .'' There was a pause as if he were checking a watch, say, or a wall clock. ''One hour. One hour to decide.''

''Look, O'Grady, I . . . .''

''Inside one hour you will call this number.'' He read it off in a series of clipped syllables. ''You will tell the person who answers that you have capitulated. If he has not received this message I shall release the Spore. It will be released from a maximum dispersion point, by the most effective means possible. You already know what the consequences will be.''

Hawk's voice was low and constricted. ''Yeah, I know,'' he said. ''How do I know you're not bluffing?''

''You don't,'' the voice said. ''But you dare not assume I am lying. What if I am not? Are you willing to take the chance that the ultimate destruction of all mankind rested upon a decision of yours? Because those are the stakes, Hawk. If you make the wrong decision we all die. All of us.''

''How do you know?'' Hawk said. The question had been on my own lips too.

''I've seen what happens. One of our men . . . .''

''Halloran was a phony,'' Hawk said. ''Carter killed him back in Maryland. There was no sign of the stuff on him.''

''It wasn't Halloran. One of my men was . . .

infected by the Spore. We faked the Halloran message because we couldn't use our own man. The Spore got to his face first, Hawk. By the time we found him he could no longer talk. Or think human thoughts. He had been taken over by an alien intelligence from another star. We destroyed him . . . . But not before we had seen what the Spore could do. And quickly, quickly . . . a matter of days in this case because of where the Spore struck. Take my word on the matter, Hawk. We are talking about no less than the end of the world. You have one hour. No, make that fifty-nine minutes. The clock is ticking, Hawk. Better get a decision out of the man on the other end of that hot line you've set up there in Room 405. Get it fast. You have less than an hour to decide the fate of mankind. Call the number, with the right answer, or . . . ."

Hawk put the phone down. "Goddamn it, if he's bluffing . . . if he's bluffing on us, I'll . . . ."

"Ah, but he's not," a soft voice came from the door. I shot a glance in that direction. Sinead Geoghegan stood there, her face full of stunned shock. "He's not bluffing. He has the Spore, Mr. Hawk. And he'll use it."

"Sinead!" I said. "What are you . . ."

"I—I couldn't help hearing. Your end of the conversation, I mean. You'd better take him seriously, whatever he says. What did he say?"

"The deadline's been bumped back. The decision has to be reached in one hour." I told her. Hawk was already on the hot line, dialing.

"Oh my God," she said. "One hour. And you haven't found him?"

"No. Not a lead anywhere. How do you know he isn't bluffing?"

"We caught one of them, back in Washington. After you'd left. He was one of the group who'd been detailed to destroy the body of one of the gang who had been . . . killed by the substance. Nick, he said . . . ."

"Sinead, all that means is that they've got their stories together. It could all be phony . . . ."

"No, Nick! It isn't! The man we caught . . . he had it too. My God, I almost *touched* him." Her face was full of disgust. "It was—it was awful . . . it had eaten away his throat . . . he could barely speak . . . ."

I looked at Hawk. Suddenly it was deathly quiet in the room. I shot a glance at my watch: Fifty-five minutes to the end of the world . . . .

NINETEEN

"NICK!"

Hawk's voice cut through the silence like a hot knife through soft butter. I shot him a look. So did Sinead.

"Excuse me, sir." Hawk covered up the phone speaker with one broad hand. "Nick! Sinead! Get your skull caps on. See if you can tell me how the hell O'Grady knew we were in Room 405!"

We did as neat a pair of double takes as you'll ever hope to see. We looked at Hawk—who by this time had gone back to his phone call, his brow knit, the cigar in shreds in his hand. He scowled darkly at it and heaved it, still unlit, into an ashcan.

"By God," I said. "How *did* he know? We've never mentioned the number to anybody before. He couldn't have got it off the bug because we never spoke the damn thing out loud. Mack Halloran wasn't on the circuit for this one. The only way you could get the number was through the State Department . . . and even State didn't know the location of the joint. Hmm . . . the first *I* knew of the address was when I called the number and Hawk told me where to come. The only way they could have eavesdropped on that would be if they already knew where to be."

"In other words," she said, "it couldn't be. But it is. Somehow they've broken your security. Else how . . ."

"Yeah," I said. "It doesn't make any sense." I sat down and dug inside my pocket for my cigarette case. I'd been off the stuff for a bit, but in a stress situation back came the habit again. I motioned to her with the case; she shook her head no. I lit up one of my old monogrammed filters and blew a smoke ring.

"Nick," she said, sitting down across from me and looking me in the eye. "What other handle could we catch it by? Is there another angle?"

"Hmm," I said. "There's the question of where the hell was O'Grady when he made the call. And where he is now. Damn." I got up and went over to the tape recorder that'd been monitoring the phone. I ran the tape back and replayed it:

". . . you will tell the person who answers that you have capitulated. If he has not received this message I shall release the Spore. It will be released from a maximum dispersion point, by the most effective means possible. You already know what the consequences will be . . . ."

I put one hand on the button and stopped it. Then I played it back.

". . . I shall release the Spore. It will be released from a maximum dispersion point . . . ."

I stopped it again.

"Nick!" Sinead said. "He said '*I*' shall release it. Not '*we*.' Does that tell us something?"

"It might," I said appreciatively. I looked at the clock. Forty-six minutes. "Also . . . I think he used that same phrase 'maximum dispersion' once before. Back in Sydney. Let me see if I can remember more of the conversation." I have something like 90% of total recall when I work at it. Years of training on top of the natural aptitude. I went to work on it now. "Hmmmm . . . . He said, 'where it'll get maximum dispersion. Where it'll spread to the whole city . . . within days . . .' "

She grabbed my arm with that strong little hand of hers, and I looked in her eyes now, and she had never seemed so lovely. You start to appreciate a woman, on a scale far removed from the ordinary, when you suddenly learn you stand a damn good chance of losing her. Her voice was low and husky when she said. "Nick. Go on . . . ."

"He said . . . hmm, let me see . . . 'New York will be a vast, milling mass of frightened people, trying to get out of town . . . . the Spore will get loose . . . it'll spread. . . .' "

"Yes, yes," she said. Her eyes were bright with fear and excitement. "Nick, it means they had the place planned out beforehand. And it'll be . . . it'll be centrally located . . . a place where maximum dispersion can be achieved . . . ."

"Yes," I said. "And when he called this last time O'Grady wasn't there. He'd have to *go* there. And he'd have to carry a two-way radio so they could inform him as to whether the answer we get from the president is yes or no. He . . . ."

"Nick," she said. "How do you know he wasn't there?"

I stopped and thought about that a bit. How the hell *did* I know? "Because . . . because he'll have to disperse it in the open . . . in the open air . . . from a place that's centrally located . . . a place from which the winds will carry it in all directions. . . ."

"Nick. A tall building. The World Trade Center. The tallest buildings in New York. He . . . ."

"No. Not centrally located. Hmm. Not the Chrysler either. Maybe Rockefeller Center. Yeah, possibly. But damn it, if it were there . . . why was the guy in the gray suit heading this way? No, no, he was trying to deliver the tapes to CBS, that doesn't fit . . . it *could* be Rockefeller Center. It could be . . . ."

I stopped dead. I looked at the clock. Forty minutes. No, thirty-nine. "God damn," I said. I got up and made for the door. I opened it on the fly and hit the corridor in a dead run, making for the stairs. I took them down, two and three steps at a time. I could hear her behind me. "Nick! Wait for me!"

No time to wait. I burst out into the lobby, Wilhelmina in hand. The guard was still on duty, a city cop. "Hey!" I said. "Anybody come in here in the last couple of minutes? I . . . ."

"W-why . . . only him . . . Mr. Magee, of Consolidated Opal . . . . There he goes right there . . . ."

I wheeled. Just in time to see O'Grady, looking much as I'd seen him in Sydney, standing in the express elevator, an odd-looking, bulky package perched precariously on his arm. He saw me just as the doors closed on him. Above the car door the register started to indicate the floor he was opposite . . . 2 . . . 3 . . . 4 . . .

"Nick!" Sinead said. "Wait for me!"

I wasn't waiting for anyone. I rushed to the bank of elevators and banged on the button, looking up to watch the lead he had on me . . . 16 . . . 17 . . . 18 . . . *Damn it, why won't you come? Stupid goddamn machine.*

Then she was beside me, as I watched the *down* signal sending me another elevator. "Nick! That was him, wasn't it? Wasn't it?" She grabbed my arm again, squeezing hard. Her eyes were flashing little hot lights. There was a strange flush on her face.

"Yeah," I said. "And I know where he's going. He's heading for the top. Maximum dispersion, baby. Centrally located. It's still the third highest building in the city and the winds right now are turbulent . . . they ought to spread that stuff all over . . . ." My eyes followed the *up* indicator . . . 30 . . . 31 . . . 32 . . . . Then I switched over to the *down* scale and followed that one all the way to the bottom. I shoved her roughly aside as I piled inside. I was doing my damndest to keep her the hell out of that elevator, but she wasn't having any of it.

"Sinead!" I said. "Damn it, this is dangerous. . . ."

She gave me a glare as the door closed and the car started up. "Oh, come off it," she said. "This is where we came in, after all. In an elevator, mind you. One from which *I,* poor fainting female that I am, had to rescue big fearless dashing *you.*" There was an Irish devil dancing in those angry eyes.

"Damn," I said, and let my breath out hard. "Point well taken. Are you heeled?"

She took an ugly little snubnose S&W .38 Police Special out of her shoulder purse. "Righto," she said. "And if you'll remember I can use this."

"You sure as hell can," I said with a grin. I watched her twirl the gun around her finger in a perfect roadagent's spin. "Sorry about that."

"And a good thing too," she said. "This is going to take two of us. You know that. And Nick. If you bothered to think things out you'd have to remember that if we fail in this, it won't matter anyway. We'll all be dead, and horribly so."

"Yeah," I said. "Okay, honey, you're on. And Sinead. If we get through this alive . . . ."

"Yes?" she said. Her eyes were damp. Her mouth was soft and alluring. I held out my hands to her and she melted into my arms. For a moment she was all the soft and yielding and infinitely sweet woman I'd ever met, and the fact didn't change a damn for all that she was also as tough, smart, resourceful, and ruthless a partner as I'd ever had. How in the devil had I ever thought of her as a millstone around my neck, all those days ago when we first met for a briefing back in D.C.? Now, however, she drove even that thought from my mind as she reached up and kissed me, hard, sexy, demanding. When we broke we were both breathing hard. I looked her in the eye . . . and then the car came to the end of the line.

As the door opened she said, "Is this the top?"

"No," I said. "It's the transfer point." I checked my watch again and had difficulty keeping from breaking out into a cold sweat. *Eighteen minutes to go . . .* We got in the first car that came and headed back up again.

"Look," I said, "we're going to be vulnerable the minute that door opens. Look: you get behind the operator's seat. I'll get down on the floor." I showed her, flattening out on my belly with my gun pointed at the door. "He may get me this way, but I'll get him too. If that happens, you finish him for me."

"Righto," she said. And pulled that tough-looking little revolver again. And, like me, waited for the door to open, her heart beating wildly . . . .

But at the top there was nobody waiting for us. The observation platform, as far as we could see, was empty. The wind was blowing like crazy. Below us the whole of the Island lay spread out in all its splendor and squalor. Way the hell out there you could see Jersey, way down past Richmond, halfway to Atlantic City, perhaps. You could see tankers, out to sea miles past the Narrows, skirting New York harbor, bound for Philly: nobody in his right mind would be sailing under the Verrazano Bridge on this day of all days, to dock at Brooklyn.

I stepped out onto the platform, looking up at the wire mesh they'd put up to keep jumpers from using the building. Not that it'd stopped all of them.

And all of a sudden I saw him. I yanked Wilhelmina and aimed it his way. Then I stopped.

And looked him in the eye.

"Sinead!" I said. "Put up the gun. We can't shoot."

"But Nick . . . ." she said. And then it hit her. "No, of course you're right," she said. I saw her out of the corner of my eye, putting the gun away, but it caught on something. And when it did it must have looked as though she were going to use it. O'Grady had that funny package, black and lumpy and wrapped in cloth, on his arm; with the other hand he pulled a little automatic and drilled Sinead in the shoulder. She dropped like a rock falling off a table.

I reached for Wilhelmina . . . and then put her away, cursing.

"There, there," he said. "You understand. You know you daren't shoot me. You don't know why, but you do sense something, don't you, Carter?"

"I . . . ." I looked around and down. She was out. She'd hit her head on something when the slug spun her around, and there was a trickle of blood running down that pretty cheek. "You tell me why, damn it," I said.

"Oh, it's simple," he said. There was something odd about his face . . . but then there had always been. I couldn't place what it was. The eyes were quite familiar, though. And I had no doubt that it was O'Grady. No doubt whatsoever.

"Simple," he repeated. "Simple. After all, if you shoot me it's all up for me . . . but of course it's all up for all of you, isn't it?"

"Why?" I said. "How?"

"Why, Carter, it's all quite simple. *I've got the Spore, of course*. I've got it on me. You knew that. And I'm wired up, you know. Shoot me and you will accomplish the same with your bullet that my hand will otherwise accomplish if I do not get a message in . . . hmmm . . . nine minutes, I believe. In my pocket, of course, is a button. The button will close the switch on an electrical charge which will set off an explosive secreted on my body. It will of course be the end of me. But since the Spore is on my body, it will also mean the end of all of you. All of you swine."

"O'Grady," I said, stalling, trying to think what to do. "*Why,* in God's name? What have you got against us?"

"Ah," he said, and at that precise moment I knew why. The mad glint in his eye told me. That mind of his was all shorted out. There didn't have to be a reason. If it hadn't been one thing it'd have been another. Who cared what the grudge was, how many years ago? The point was that the response to the grudge had been blown so far out of proportion by now that it almost bore no relation to the grudge any more. "Ah," he said. "You'd like to know, would you, Carter? Well, I won't tell you. Hmmm . . . seven minutes. Well, perhaps, I'll let you have some idea why, if I have to go, I don't give a damn whether or not I take you with me, all of you."

"What do you mean, O'Grady? I don't understand. What do you mean, if you have to go? Who says you have to go? Look, call this thing off and I'll work out a plea bargain for you. I'll . . . ."

The eyes were full of a wild glint of pure and undiluted hatred . . . but the face . . . the face stayed impassive. The mouth hardly moved at all. "Plea bargain? What use would I have for one of those, Carter? Can you give me back the life I wasted? Can you give me back the youth I squandered, fighting the British, slaving like a dog to rid the Island of the damned Sassenach swine that infested her? Always in the hope—the vain hope—of a better life? Always in the forlorn hope that something I might do would make a better world for me and mine? Can you?''

''Here!'' said a weak voice behind me. I half-whirled to see Sean Mulrae, standing with one hand on the guide rail. His face was barely on the pink side of white; I could see under his open jacket the red stains showing through his shirt. I hadn't any idea how he'd come up here, but he'd damn near killed himself doing so. His face was an icy mask of hatred. ''Here!'' he said. ''What is all this talk of you and yours, you dog?'' He reached inside the bloodstained jacket and pulled a little Spanish pistol—7mm, from the look of it.

''Who are you?'' O'Grady said.

''Who am I?'' Sean said in a high-pitched voice full of loathing. ''The bastard you left on Norah Mulrae twenty-nine years ago, you son of a whore!'' He started to say something else, but he was interrupted by a fit of coughing. ''I . . . I've sworn to kill you . . . I've carried the secret around for seven years now . . . and now it all doesn't matter. None of the hopes and dreams my mother had for me, none of the hopes I had of a lasting peace in the land . . . none of them matters a damn. What does matter is that I'm going to kill you. Kill you with these two hands of mine . . . .''

''Stay back!'' O'Grady said. ''Stay back or . . . or I'll press the button. I'll . . . .'' His eyes suddenly registered surprise. Then, a faint smile crossing his face, he reached across his body and yanked the black cloth off the bundle on his arm.

Mulrae stopped in his tracks.

The falcon on O'Grady's arm was hooded. Its beak was curved and sharp; the talons that encircled O'Grady's coat sleeve were like little razors. O'Grady's hand went to the falcon's hood; then stayed.

"You know," he said. "If I take off this hood he'll go for one of you—the closest to him. He'll have no mercy. He'll tear you to ribbons. He'll rip your eyes out, tear your face to shreds . . . ."

Mulrae had stopped dead, his near hand inside his jacket, pressed to the red spot on the bandages. He was gasping for breath at this height; his mouth was open and his head drooped slightly. I didn't figure him for having much stamina left.

"Three minutes," O'Grady said. "No, make that two. And then? Do you want to know what'll happen then? Let me show you! Let me demonstrate for you what will be the fate of the world that's betrayed me so! Let me show you!"

His free hand went to his face. He'd stashed the little gun somewhere. My eyes searched for it. But then they went back to his face. To the fingers that slowly peeled the plastic face mask away, an inch at a time . . . .

"Jesus, Mary and Joseph." Mulrae said in a hoarse voice.

Under the false skin was the real one.

It was gray, all gray: doughy and puffy, with a

strange spongy texture. The gray spread all the way up from his collar past his mouth—it was a featureless slash by now—to his cheeks. It stopped just below his eyes. The gray flesh was dead, unfeeling, unresponsive.

"You see?" O'Grady said. "I'm all over like that now. All over below the cheeks. All over. And that's the way you'll all look. All of you. All four billion of you. Every last man, woman and child on this godforsaken, heartless globe. All gray, gray like me . . . ."

TWENTY

THERE WAS A moment of silence. Nothing but the wind wailing away, up there at the top of the world; nothing but the stray cry of a bird, soaring past, and the hooded falcon stirring restlessly; nothing but the beating of my own heart. I shot the bird a glance; then I looked hard at O'Grady's horrible features and the mad eyes, full of hatred and pain. For a moment all I could think of was, *the poor son of a bitch*. Then I remembered where we were, and why we were there, and the hair stood up on the back of my neck and the adrenaline was up, and every nerve was awake and alive. My mind raced at breakneck speed. What if . . . . Mulrae laughed, harshly. The laugh turned to a cough. I looked his way; there was a trickle of blood running down his jaw from a corner of his mouth. "Ah, there, O'Grady," he said. "Then we're in the same boat, you bastard. You're going to die, I'm going to die. Whatever I do up here I won't survive it. I made it out of the hospital all right, and I made my way here. But it's finished me. A minute left, you say? Even if you *do* what you say you're going to, it won't matter a damn to me. I've got perhaps a half hour to go anyway. And I've lived for nothing else than this moment for years. Do you think I'm going to let you cheat me of it? Cheat me of the pleasure of wrapping these hands of mine around that filthy neck of yours and strangling the life out of you, before I'm done? If you do you forget one thing." His voice was low—you wouldn't think it would carry, with that wind going—but you could make out every syllable he said. There was an edge on it that would cut glass.

"Forget what?" O'Grady said. The voice shook.

"That I'm my father's son," Mulrae said, and his voice held self-loathing and despair that I'll carry with me to my dying day. "And I don't give a damn about any concerns but my own. And my concern right now—my last concern, father o' mine—is ridding the earth of the likes of yourself.'' A ghastly smile on his face, he edged forward. I looked down at his hands. They wore gloves, and blood had dripped down into one of them, staining it. They clenched and unclenched. ''Do your worst, O'Grady. What do I care . . . .''

O'Grady's eyes, the only part of him that could register emotion any more, showed abject fear. He backed off and clawed with his free hand at the hood on the falcon.

Just as his fingers pulled the hood loose Mulrae, in a voice that was like the bellow of an enraged ox, yelled: *''Nick! Grab the bird!''*

And he dived for O'Grady, those gloved hands outstretched.

And the bird headed straight for his face.

I shot across that intervening space with lightening speed. I got one arm in front of his face just in time for the bird's flashing talons to sweep down on it and rip my sleeve right down to the wrist. The wings beat wildly; the curved beak sliced away at my face.

I grabbed those mighty little legs, getting my palms sliced up badly for my pains, and hung on for dear life. The wings battered the air savagely; the beak hunted for my eyes and caught me above the eyebrow, a sudden rush of blood trailing down into one eye. I shook my head, wondering how the hell to let go of this thing. And out of the corner of my free eye I could see Mulrae, his gloved hands on O'Grady's wrists, grappling with the strange gray creature. Mulrae was weak from loss of blood, and O'Grady's no longer earthly muscles held a superhuman strength. He struggled mightily, trying to get one hand free so that he could reach for the button—the fatal button—in his pocket.

The bird nearly tore my ear off with the next swipe of that wicked beak. I looked away from Mulrae and ducked another vicious attack.

And then I got my second wind. And all of a sudden my foggy head was clear, and there wasn't but one thing to do.

Holding the falcon by the ankles, I swung him around as hard as I could, with those wings beating away like that, and whammed him into the wall.

It stunned him slightly; the wings stopped their frantic waving. I swung again. This time his nasty little head took the full force of the wallop, bamming into the wall as hard as I could swing him.

The taloned legs I was holding relaxed a little. Just enough to let me shake Hugo out into one palm and cut the bird's throat.

He struggled; they have strength to spare even after they're technically dead . . . but he all of a sudden went into a last spasm and collapsed.

I drew Wilhelmina. I don't think I've ever drawn faster. But even as I reached for her I could see O'Grady rip his hands free from Mulrae, stagger back, and reach for that all-important pocket.

There was a shot. Just one.

And right in the middle of O'Grady's forehead,

virtually the only flesh-colored part of his body any more, a red flower blossomed. The light went out of his eyes forever. And, like a puppet whose strings have been cut, he pitched forward on his face, in a splash of blood.

With a shudder Mulrae stepped back, careful not to let the body touch him as it fell.

I closed my eyes, hoping against hope . . . . but the thing didn't go off. I let out a deep breath and leaned back against the wall. Looking behind me I said, "Sinead?" fully expecting to see her coming off the floor, smoking pistol in one pretty hand, with those Irish eyes blazing.

But the person with the gun was David Hawk. And for once in his life those bulldog jaws weren't clamped around a cigar. The mouth was grim, but the eyes held a note of relief. Of triumph. Finally, of jubilation.

Then he caught himself showing emotion and scowled. He returned the gun to the firing-range's "ready" position, pointing it at the sky. And only then did he shoot me a glance.

"Well, Carter?" he said, and dug into a pocket with his free hand for a cigar. "Don't just stand there. One would think you'd never seen a good shot before."

Good shot? Of course I had. I'd been on the range with Hawk. He could draw a bead on a guy standing behind plate glass 300 yards away, firing through a windstorm and a heavy rain, and shoot the ash off the guy's cigarette without putting out the smoke. But if he lived to be 105 he'd never make a better shot than that one, or a more important one.

Shot! "Jesus Christ," I said. "Sinead . . . ."

But Mulrae was even faster on the uptake than I was. He'd shucked the gloves, his jacket, his shirt—everything about him that could possibly have touched O'Grady's tainted flesh—and had bent to pick her up carefully, gently. As he straightened up, the bandage around his chest still stained with his own blood, I marveled at the stamina of the man. "Mulrae," I said. "For God's sake hand her here. You're hurt . . . ."

"Ah, Carter," he said, a Mick grin cutting across his face. "You'd be after believing a bunch of Irish bullshit? I'm out of the hospital all right, but on a clean bill of health. I had to blather a bit, for O'Grady's sake, until I could figure out what to do." And he carried her over to the elevator.

"Well, I'll be damned," I said.

Hawk had the cigar plugged into his kisser now. "No," he said. "That's the whole point of today, Nick—that you won't. And I won't. And none of us will."

"What?" I said. I stowed my little arsenal away, looking down at the dead bird, then looking out over the city and the harbor. "What do you mean?"

"I mean it's all over. The Guard's down in the streets, restoring order. There's an Airborne unit coming across from Jersey to spell them. There's. . . ."

"Hey," I said. "But the Spore? What if they have more of it? What if it's too late?"

"I got a call from the White House. They've isolated a powerful antibody. There's a counter-strain. It's fatal to the Spore organism in all cases. The stuff's in massive production right now—just in case. Shots are going to be available to everybody in a matter of days."

I let out another deep breath.

"Come on," Hawk said. "This case is closed. And three minutes after the president's call came in, he called back. There's another emergency brewing. Somewhere in Africa, as I remember. . . ."

I looked at him hard. The mouth was hard as usual, but the eyes were smiling. "Okay," I said. "Let's go."

TWENTY-ONE

TWENTY-FOUR HOURS later, all briefed, I jogged down the corridor to the loading deck, looking hard at the wall clock and wondering if I were late. They'd dumped me off at the airport after a fast ride in a big, powerful car, and if the wall clock was right I was still two minutes off schedule. I stepped up the pace . . . and then stopped dead about ten feet from the ramp. There they were, blocking my way, both of them. And from the looks of things the plane wasn't going anywhere. Not for a moment or two, anyway.

I looked the both of them over. Mulrae's wide-open, round, redheaded kisser was positively beaming. His arm was thrown protectively around Sinead's slender shoulders. His touch, where the sling went over one shoulder, was empathetic and gentle.

"You know, damn it," I said, "I thought you two were the biggest pain in the ass I ever had when I first met you. Now . . . ."

"Yes, I know," Sinead said. Her black-Irish smile was dazzling, for all that her face seemed a little wan. "And we thought that way about each other at first as well. But . . . ."

"But all that proves," Mulrae finished the thought for her, "is that a man doesn't always know his own mind."

"Or a woman either," she said. "Nick . . . ."

"Hey, wait a minute," I said. "Is this real?"

"You never know where lightning is going to strike," she said, her eyes affectionately on mine. "And Nick, the one thing all this has brought home to us is that it all has to stop, the fighting between North and South, between Orange and Green. . . ."

"So we're going home to work to end it," Mulrae said. "And we'll do it, anyhow, sooner or later. Just you watch."

"I wouldn't be surprised," I said. "Anybody who can stop O'Grady's crowd can stop anything. Good luck." I shook his hand . . . but Sinead would have none of this handshake business. She slipped forward and put as much as she could into a strong little one-handed hug, that powerful little arm around my neck, and kissed me with feeling. Feeling? The Irish invented the word. I winked at the both of them and slipped into the covered ramp leading its way down into the big jet. In my window seat I saw them wave once before walking away, so close together you could get the two of them in the same overcoat.

The stewardess, a fresh-faced type with the most amazing long legs, fussed happily about, tucking me in. "I'm sorry I kept everybody waiting," I said. "I . . . ."

"That's all right," she said. "I mean you weren't the one we were waiting for."

I gulped. I did a double take. And then I looked up and saw what she meant. And who would they hold up a whole 747 for, bound for Kinshasa? Who but N21—the new operative we'd taken on the night before to replace Terry Considine.

I looked N21 over. Well, I'd had worse partners on a job before. And for all that Terry Considine's shoes would be hard for anybody short of Superman to fill, I figured I'd do all right with this one.

N21? How about tall and regal, with a short Afro hairdo that framed the face of a brown-eyed Nefretete with a skin the color of a Hershey bar without almonds? How about red lips and white teeth and gold hoops in the ears, and the most amazing body you ever laid eyes on.

As she sat down I got a little shock. I winced.

She did too. "Hey, baby," she said. "This joint is full of static . . . ."

I let that long thigh slide down mine and felt her hand on my arm. The electricity was still there. "No it isn't, Mamie," I said. "Remind me to explain later."

Her grin was carnal and appreciative. "Explain hell, Carter," she said. "Demonstrate." She patted my hand. "That's all right. I can wait until Kinshasa . . . ."

Underneath us the big jets roared to life. The doors closed. The red lights went on. Slowly we started taxiing down the runway. The electricity was still running up and down my thigh. "That's fine," I said. "I wonder if *I* can . . . ."

BE SURE TO READ THE NEXT
ALL NEW NICK CARTER ADVENTURE

THE ASIAN MANTRAP

From a Washington, D.C. meeting of the Strategic Operations Board to the deadly heart of Hanoi, North Vietnam, Nick pursues a renegade hero–General Keith Martin–who has some old debts to collect. Is Martin on a personal vendetta? Or was he brainwashed in a POW camp? Whatever the answer, Martin has to be stopped. And Nick Carter, with the help of a beautiful and deadly Eurasian agent, is the man for the job!

On either side of the table were a man and a woman, Caucasians, who stared at the intruder in blank shock. Immediately in front of him was a thin-necked Vietnamese woman in traditional national dress. The gunman froze. Huong, formerly general in charge of all military security and prisoner-of-war confinements during the Vietnam War, was supposed to be alone.

He had an impulse to flee, but at that instant the chunky figure of Minister Huong, who was facing the intruder, rose to his feet. Huong's sudden movement was like that of a pop-up silhouette target on a firing range where the gunman had practiced to react against this very contingency.

Suddenly calm, he leveled his weapon and sprayed the minister with a short, accurate burst. Huong had just started to dive under the table when the slugs caught him in the chest.

The killer fired continuously, raking the room from right to left. The chatter of the pistol hardly missed a beat as he removed the clip and inserted the second loaded one. The Vietnamese woman's head dropped to one side suddenly, the muscles and arteries in her neck severed. The European, in a tailored dinner jacket, remained sitting upright, but his head sank slowly as if to comtemplate the stitchings of blood welling and spreading on his shirt front.

The woman across the table was halfway to her feet with her mouth open to scream when the deadly bullets stifled her. A single whistling gasp escaped from her before blood gushed from her throat and she was flung loosely upon the chair, at once painting its needlepoint a bright crimson.

As he retreated slowly through the streets of

Hanoi he evaluated his mission: nothing had gone wrong except that Huong should have been alone; but four go as easily as one at close range. Besides the Vietnamese woman and the two Europeans were in the way of the assignment.

He wondered who the two Caucasians were.

Neither one had had a chance to speak.

And now they never would, which was all to the good.

Dead men tell no tales.

Besides, he told himself again, they were in the way of a mission he'd vowed to carryout to the end, no matter what the cost.